THE FALL OF THE ANGEL
NATHALIE
JAMIE BRINDLE

BEDLAM PRESS
2012

First Edition Trade Paperback

THE FALL OF THE ANGEL NATHALIE
© 2013 by Jamie Brindle
Cover art © 2013 by Travis Anthony Soumis

This edition © 2013 Bedlam Press

ISBN: 978-1-939065-21-6

Assistant Editors:
Amanda Baird
C. Dennis Moore

Book design & typesetting:
David G. Barnett
Fat Cat Graphic Design
www.fatcatgraphicdesign.com

Bedlam Press
an imprint of
Necro Publication
5139 Maxon Terrace
Sanford, FL 32771
www.necropublications.com

10 9 8 7 6 5 4 3 2 1

To the real Nathalie, of course, however different she is from the one in my story; and to Snelsmore Common, where the first pages were written one sunny day almost ten years ago.

I would like to thank all my family and friends who helped in the proofreading process: Marian Brindle, Roxanne Hirons, Charlotte Warren, Daniel Davies, and everyone else whose feedback helped address false starts and wrong turns. Also many thanks to Garreth Hirons, who helped me identify the lyrics I wished I could have started each section with, if only I could have got copyright...and to my favourite band for writing them. I would also like to thank my beautiful girlfriend Chloe, for her forbearance in granting me the hours spent in front of a computer monitor, as well as for her spirited attempt at drawing an angel.

Many thanks are also due to Scotopia Press, and in particular, to Molly Feese, who helped me with my first proper taste of editorial feedback, when they published the first part of this story in their *Dark Distortions* anthology back in 2008.

Finally, of course, many thanks to Dave B. at Necro/Bedlam for the chance to get this out there, and to Travis Soumis for the great cover art.

PART ONE

Outside the sun was shining brightly, but Julie had pulled the curtains closed, and the metal in her hand felt cold. She adjusted her skirt, glanced at the clock, and poured herself another drink. It was too early to be drinking—a little over half past three in the afternoon—but Julie couldn't stop thinking about what it would be like when the door opened, and she didn't want her hand shaking when he walked in. She wanted it to be clean.

She owed the cheating bastard that much.

The drink went back in one shot, and burnt her all the way down to her belly. She had never been a big whisky drinker. Never been a big anything drinker. But today was different. It wasn't every day you decided to terminate ten years of marriage down a barrel.

She slammed the glass down onto the table and looked at the letters again. She'd read them each at least a dozen times, and knew them by heart. But she couldn't stop. They were too satisfying; they were a certification of her sanity.

She ran the conversation in her head again. October last year:

-Where do you go to see her?

-What?

-Where do you see her, I said. Her place? A hotel? *Here*?

-I don't know what you're talking about.

-Stop it! Stop pretending!

-I'm not pretending about anything! I don't know what you're talking about.

-Screw you! I found them!

-What? What did you find?

-Your stupid goddamn letters to your stupid goddamn whore! They're right there. You could have at least taken the time to hide them. It's almost like you wanted me to find them!

-Julie, I honestly don't know what you're talking about. Why are you talking like this?

-Open the drawer. Just open the drawer, and show me what's inside.

-There's nothing inside.

-Then open it.

-There. See. A letter from my cousin. Another one from the bank. Jesus, Julie! Haven't we been through this a thousand times before?

-They were there, they were right there! I saw them. I fucking saw them. I was looking at them ten minutes ago!

-Julie, have you been skipping your meds again? You know you gotta take those things. You *know* it. Now listen. I'm not gonna get angry. We both know that wouldn't do any good. But please, please. Keep taking the pills, OK? Please.

«‹‹—››»

Keep taking the pills. She hated that more than the lies. That stupid, lousy holier-than-thou calmness. How could he do that to her? How could he have made her doubt herself? Just so that he could carry on screwing that slut of a secretary. Was that all her sanity was worth? A few animal minutes with a skinny little bimbo with no brains? That brought a wry smile to her lips. At least *she* had enough brains to go crazy. That whore of his didn't even have that. It wouldn't be possible for someone as vacuous as that to go insane. There wasn't enough brains in that empty head of hers to split into different personalities. If she heard voices, she wouldn't even bother to let them speak; she'd be too busy waxing lyrical about her latest hairdo.

Still, Julie would soon see what brains the slut had in that little head of hers. She'd put them all over the wall, right next to the brains of that lying worthless husband of hers. She'd decided before she'd finished reading the first letter. This was a more recent one. It had been dated last January. Three months after she'd found the others. She still didn't know how he'd managed to swap them for the innocent letters he'd pulled out of the drawer when she'd confronted him. But that didn't matter now. What mattered now was that it was twenty minutes past four, and Stan thought she was at her mother's house for the weekend, and in ten minutes or so he'd come waltzing in through the front door with that slut of his. What mattered now was that she'd checked that the gun was loaded five times. She was no hotshot, but you didn't need to be from five feet away.

She didn't care anymore that she had run out of pills a week ago.

What mattered now was having another drink.

She poured herself a shot—emptied the bottle in fact—and raised the glass to her lips.

She was just about to knock it back, when something flickered outside the window, like a cloud darting in front of the sun. Julie frowned and put the glass down again, untouched. A shiver ran through her body, and she had the strangest feeling that somehow, something was not normal, just not right.

Then, with a scraping of gravel, a car pulled into the driveway, and Julie forgot all about it. He was here.

She swallowed. Her heart was beating like a drum. She tried to control her breathing, but it came in ragged, shallow gasps.

There were footsteps on the drive, leading up to the door. They stopped.

She licked her lips. Any second now. The key would turn in the lock, and he would walk in, and she would shoot him.

It took all her effort to hold the gun steady.

She waited.

But there was no sound of a key being inserted into a lock. Instead, there was a gentle knocking at the door.

Julie frowned. She was not expecting anybody other than Stan. No one came to see *her*. Even the Jehovah's Witnesses had learnt to give *this* house a wide berth.

Cautious, she moved towards the door.

"Yes," she called, and was surprised by how steady she managed to make her voice.

"Julie?" came a voice. Muffled as it was through the door, Julie knew that it wasn't her husband. It was a woman's voice.

"Yes," she answered. "What do you want?"

"My name's Nathalie. Nathalie…" The woman said her last name, but just at that moment a lorry rumbled past on the road outside, and Julie couldn't make it out.

"I work with your husband," the woman who called herself Nathalie went on. "I've got a message from him. Can I come in?"

"Wait a moment," Julie called. She didn't want anyone to see her like this.

She rushed back into the kitchen and put away the whisky bottle and the glass. She slid the letters under her chair, and hid the gun in a drawer. Then she ran back to the front door, unbolted it, and opened it wide to the sunlight.

Julie had to squint. Outside stood a slender young woman. She had shoulder-length brown hair, glistening in the sun, and a pale blue dress that flowed down to her feet.

"I'm so sorry to bother you," said the lady, "but I have some urgent news from your husband. Do you mind if I sit and talk with you a while?"

Nathalie's voice had a strange lilt to it, but Julie could not place it.

She hesitated before allowing the woman into her house. What if her husband came back while they were talking? Then she realized that if this woman had come with some message from her husband it was unlikely that he would turn up while a woman spoke on his behalf

She opened the door and stood aside. Nathalie smiled and walked in.

The room seemed dark after the brilliant daylight outside. Julie moved in a daze, and bumped into a stool before she could sit on it. Strange that the only thing in the room that seemed bright enough was Nathalie. The woman seemed to *glow*.

"So," Julie said, falling on the stool, "do you know Stan well?"

"I see him from time to time." she answered with a little smile. "But I'm not a close friend, no."

"Oh." said Julie. All of a sudden her head felt heavy. Her belly felt a little sick from the whisky. "Well, how come he sent you here with a message then?"

"He didn't send me," answered Nathalie.

Julie waited for the woman to go on, but she just sat there smiling at her.

Julie blinked. Her mouth was full of a sour taste. She was aware of the sound of another car pulling into the drive, but it seemed far away, and not at all important.

"Then why are you here? You said you had a message from him," she managed to say, after swallowing back bile.

"I came to tell you that he loves you," Nathalie said.

Julie frowned. This wasn't the type of message she was expecting. Could Stan have realized that she'd found his wretched letters? Had he hired Nathalie to try and sweet talk her? If only she could think!

There was a rushing sound in her ears. What was wrong with her?

"He loves me, huh?" Julie half-mumbled. "Yeah, sure he does. Almost as much as he loves that slut secretary of his."

"Stanley doesn't have a secretary," Nathalie countered, firm but not unkind. "He hasn't had one for three months, not since he quit his job at Harts, and went to work in the timber yard. He gave up his job because you were always imagining that he was…having relations with his co-workers. Don't you remember, Julie? Think. He quit. Remember? He quit for you."

Julie frowned.

THE FALL OF THE ANGEL NATHALIE

That was right, wasn't it? Stan *had* quit. He had said they wouldn't be able to afford to go out so much any more, on account of the pay wasn't so good down at the timber yard. Yes, that was right…but then, who was the letter from?

Julie screwed up her eyes. If only she could *think*. *Of course* Stan had quit his job. She *knew* that. How could she have forgotten? She shook her head, but the cobwebs stuck firm there. Why did nothing seem to make sense?

There was the sound of a key rattling in the front door. Julie felt every muscle in her body tighten. Her heart was beating hard again. Stan was back.

Nathalie was still in the room, but somehow she seemed to fade, to recede into the background and become less important.

Julie opened the drawer and pulled out the gun. She staggered to her feet just as the door opened and Stan walked in.

He took in the gun, the look in her eyes. He froze.

"Oh, Julie," he said.

Her hand wavered. The gun moved up and down, shaking a little.

"If he loves me, why did he do this to me?" she muttered. Her finger tightened on the trigger.

"He has done nothing to you but love you," Nathalie whispered. She was standing very close to Julie's ear, but her words were quiet, a breath of warm air against her shoulder.

"Oh, Julie," he said again, and it wasn't him she wanted to shoot anymore.

She turned the barrel so quick Stan had no time to move. She didn't aim it properly, but it was pointing at her face when she pulled the trigger.

Julie felt the breath of air as the gun jerked in her hand.

Stan didn't even shout, he just surged forward.

Julie was on the floor, blood streaming from her face and staining the white carpet when he reached her. She was panting. The bullet had only grazed her cheek, but she was in shock.

She coughed and coughed, and when Stan helped her to sit up, she threw up a gut full of whisky and sickness onto the floor.

12

The door was open, and they were alone. A breeze blew in from outside and ruffled some blank pieces of paper out from under one of the chairs. They were creased and folded.

Stan held her tight, and when she could talk she told him that she needed to go to the hospital. Her cheek had stopped bleeding, but that didn't matter, she told him, because that's not why she had to go to the hospital.

«««——»»»

"You shouldn't take such risks," muttered Aekmar. "If they were to find out, I dread to think what would happen to you!"

Nathalie laughed.

"*If* they find out?" she exclaimed. "Are you suggesting our most glorious masters are anything less than omniscient? What faith you have! How becoming that is in an Angel!"

Aekmar looked quite serious.

"You know what I mean, young one, so do not play your little games with me! And do stop pouting, it quite spoils your clever words!"

They were walking together through the Gardens of Avalon. The sun was shining bright and beautiful as ever, and under their bare feet the grass was soft and cool. Here and there other Angels walked one by one or in little groups.

"One small breath, that was all!" Nathalie protested. "It hardly touched their world. It barely moved an atom."

"On the contrary, it moved many millions of atoms," Aekmar grimaced. "You were never very interested in their science, were you? Do you know how many atoms there are in a bullet?"

Nathalie made a face.

"What of their science?" she said. "I know how many Angels can sit on the head of a pin, that should be enough for anyone."

"Oh, be serious for a moment, will you?" Aekmar stopped walking, and caught her arm. "Yes, you are right, they knew what you did. How could they not? But do you know how close they were to issuing a decree? Of course you don't! Not you! When have you ever had time for such things? But I was there, I was watching just as they were; and what you committed was Intervention!"

Nathalie raised a dainty thumb and forefinger, and held them no more than a shade apart.

"An itsy bitsy little breath of air, that's all," she said, a look of mock surprise on her face. "What would you have done, let her shoot herself?"

"It was *Intervention*!" Aekmar hissed, ignoring her question. "And an inch or mile hardly matters with such crimes; you could get *cut* for less!"

Nathalie laughed, a beautiful tinkling sound that rippled through the trees and seemed to make the sun shine even brighter for a moment.

"Oh, Aekmar, there's no need to be so melodramatic," she giggled. "They're hardly likely to wheel out the old Hecatomb for such a little thing!"

Aekmar tightened his grip.

"How can you speak of such things?" he fretted. "Here, in Avalon, how can you speak of it?"

"I simply open my mouth, and the words come out," she laughed, refusing to be drawn into her friend's worries. "Now come, let's forget this nonsense, and have a glass of wine to celebrate!"

"I don't see what there is to celebrate." Aekmar sounded dour. "She flouts the rules we've lived by for ten thousand years and mocks the most terrible creation in all of Heaven—both in the same day, I might add—and decides that this is something to celebrate! What times we live in!"

"What have we got to celebrate?" Nathalie sounded scandalized. "Why, a hundred thousand clients—a hundred thousand souls we have been sent to save, and a hundred percent success rate of course! Isn't that enough for you?"

Aekmar shrugged, and took her arm.

"Well, I suppose it's enough," he said, relenting. "I just hope it's enough for you. Maybe next time you'll have the sense to lose a client before you risk losing your wings."

Nathalie nodded, mock serious.

"Maybe, maybe," she said.

Arm in arm, they walked through the garden.

Below her, the world spun lazily on its axis. Clouds drifted and swirled across the continents, and in the dark half of the globe millions of lights shone like motes of dust in the moonlight. Nathalie stood in the shadows and looked on. This room always filled her with wonder. How incredible the world was. How beautiful and terrible and ugly and divine. She half closed her eyes, and quested towards the planet. Her awareness brushed over the continents, skimmed the sea, streaked the air. She pressed against it all; she felt a million heartbeats, in cities, in ships, in aeroplanes, all over the world. She could rush towards any of them. She could hone in on any individual in the space between two breaths. She allowed herself to probe a little deeper into the lives she touched: she felt pain and joy, jealousy, pride, love. It was all here, every shade of human emotion, like a vast book open before her. There were so many beautiful things down below, her heart became swollen and tender. But there were many wicked things there, too, and they desiccated her like a dry wind.

She longed to pluck them away. But they were like weeds in the garden, and no matter how hard she and the other angels tried to cut them back they would always sprout again. Even if you cut away the roots, new seeds were always springing into life. And it did not help that angels were not permitted to use their own hands. Oh, how much easier that would be! How frustrating this task could be—convincing flowers to pull up thistles! Well, the others might refrain from so much as blowing a breath of air, but she would not bind herself as tight as them, no matter what Aekmar said. She did not care what the letter of Divine Law said—she followed its essence, she was certain of that much. And who got the job done with greater skill than she?

THE FALL OF THE ANGEL NATHALIE

She shook herself. Well, the garden would not become cleaner with her in torpor, contemplating, agonising. What should she do next?

She turned her attention once more to the world. There was so much to choose from—but in a way it did not matter where one began. Better to plunge in and get to work.

She streamed in towards the globe. All around her she felt the hum of agony and temptation; she picked a mote at random and focussed on it, until the rest faded away and were lost to the background. The room began to falter around her as she sunk into the world. She closed her eyes, and when she opened them again she was back on Earth.

«‹—›»

This room was dank and dark. Not filled with reverential shadows like the Room of the World, where she had been before. Those were shadows designed to stop the attention being distracted from what was of true import. No, these shadows were made to stop people seeing what they were not meant to see. In these shadows, one could hardly see oneself.

Nathalie stretched and tried to work out where she was. The descent from Heaven always made her stiff and tired. She seemed to be in some kind of small anteroom. One tiny window near the ceiling let in a little light, but it seemed dirty and second hand. A metal grill covered the opening. There was one old wooden chair next to a small dressing table with a smudged mirror and a few small drawers. On the surface there were some pots of makeup and cheap perfume. In one corner there was a little pile of clothes, dresses, panties, a bra. A single door led out of the room. Someone was out there. She could hear them breathing. She drifted to the door and peered around it.

The door led into a bedroom, not as tiny as the room she had first arrived in, but still small. There was a larger window in here. The curtains were drawn, but Nathalie could see a lattice of bars silhouetted against the daylight, visible through the thin cloth.

An electric lamp burned orange in one corner of the room. It was a very bare space, like a hotel room, anonymous and without life. A man was dressing himself at the foot of the bed. A young woman lay on the bed, naked apart from where a corner of the blanket had been pulled over her shoulders. Her pale skin looked sallow in the sour light leaking in between the curtains.

Nathalie hung in the shadows. Being gentle, she pressed her mind against the two humans, using one of those fine talents which Angels are permitted to wield. From the man she sensed a warm satisfaction, mixed with the traces of a guilt that he seemed to be suppressing with practiced skill. The woman was more difficult. Her mind was closed very tight, and difficult to open. Nathalie was skilful, however, and with some persistence she managed to seep inside. Her awareness moved like a vapor into the woman's thoughts.

Nathalie was horrified at what she found there.

The woman's mind was like the room itself, bare and empty, a gutted ship. She held no feelings; a few thoughts skittered idly thorough this hollow space. She left the thoughts unexamined and probed deeper. At last she found something, coiled tight and held fast so that it could not escape. Nathalie unravelled the feelings with tenderness and examined them. She was not surprised by what she found. Fear, and pain, and loneliness; and held especially tight, as if the girl thought this one most dangerous and most likely to escape, a twisted knot of bright red anger, loathing even, so fierce it burnt Nathalie when she brushed against it; she dropped it and it sprung back into place.

Nathalie frowned. Gently, she withdrew from the girl. That is what she was: not a woman, but a girl. The man finished tightening a tie around his neck, and began smoothing down his jacket. He was about to leave. Or rather, that's what he thought he was going to do. Nathalie smiled. Well, perhaps he would. That remained to be seen. Right now, she needed more time. That was no problem. Angels, of course, have all the time in the world.

Nathalie raised an eyebrow, and the man's hand stopped in the act of brushing his jacket. The girl's chest froze still as ice, her breath caught short. In this silence that was left once time had departed, they both looked to be halfway between death and sleep.

"What a pretty trick," exclaimed a voice three inches from her ear. "Did you learn it from a book or find it in a Christmas cracker?"

«‹‹—››»

Nathalie re-crossed her legs for the hundredth time, and blew a puff of smoke into the frozen room. She watched with vague interest as the smoke billowed away from her and then froze as it entered the sphere of timelessness she had cast around the bed. She snorted and stubbed the cigarette out on the sole of her shoe.

"Ghastly thing," she muttered. "I thought you were a life-long non-smoker? You always used to upbraid me when I so much as looked at a cigarette!"

"True; but that was before I got this rather nice body. So many bits are *nearly* human; I could no longer stand the temptation. Which led me to wonder," Jason went on, leaning forward so that his face was very close, "why it was that you were always so keen on the bloody things, eh?"

Nathalie rolled her eyes.

"I began to get the impression I was a bit too angelic-looking for my own good." she said. "No one's ready to trust someone who looks too perfect. Purely for effect, I assure you."

"Oh, they brought you down to earth you mean," said Jason. "A similar thing happened to me: once I got brought down to earth, I couldn't get enough of them."

Nathalie sighed aloud.

"Why do I get the feeling I'm heading towards *another* lecture on the rules of Intervention?" she asked.

Jason spread his arms in defence.

"Hey, come on now," he protested. "Don't think for a moment that those upstairs are the only ones keeping an eye on you. Matter of fact, you're quite a dinner-table subject here on Earth, too."

"Really? You mean you have time for that in between laying temptations and corrupting people?"

"Wow, I mean, Nathalie, sweetheart, let's not get personal here, huh?"

"I won't if you won't,"

"Ok, fair point. But all I'm saying is, I don't mix business and pleasure. And when we've got time off, you are a major source of entertainment, baby!"

"Don't call me baby. I'm three thousand years old."

"Look, baby, honeybun, sweetheart, *darling*...You know, I'd hate to see you throw three thousand years of good work down the drain just because you're tired of getting the pawns to do the work."

"Like you did, you mean," her voice was cold. "How are the scars, Jason? Is it true you get phantom-pains, like any other amputee?"

Jason stared at her for a moment, then burst out laughing.

"I've got to hand it to you, Nat: for a certified angel, you'd make one hell of a good player for our team. Hey, you sure you haven't got some kind of demon's *tongue* in that head of yours? You know, if I hadn't already got money riding on you, I'd be *rooting* for you to push things further. We could really do with someone like you down here!"

Nathalie found herself laughing too, and for a moment it was just like the old days.

"They're running *bets* on if I'm going to Intervene or not?" she asked, incredulous.

"Well, not exactly. Everyone *knows* you're going to Intervene. The bet is whether you're going to get cut for it or not."

The laughter died down a little. Nathalie found herself looking at Jason's shoulders under his well-tailored suit. Could she make out faint bulges there? Little slight lumps under the fabric, where before there had been...? She remembered how beautiful he used to look, with his ebony hair and emerald feathers. But that was so long ago, before he became greedy, before he slipped...

THE FALL OF THE ANGEL NATHALIE

She coughed, and suddenly she didn't feel like laughing anymore.

After some few moments of silence, Nathalie indicated the man frozen by the bed in the act of dressing, and said, "So, he comes here to rape the girl often?"

Jason's smile had faded, too.

"About, uh, once a week," he said. "He's not the only one. This young lady is well provided for, you might say. Madam downstairs sees to that. One of her most popular girls. Why, you here to save him?"

Nathalie's lips tightened.

"Maybe I've thought about it," she snapped.

"He's beyond it, believe me," said Jason, with a curious mixture of pride and shame. "He's...well he's one of my best clients."

Nathalie stared at him, until Jason went on.

"Matter of fact, that's why I'm here now. That lump in his suit," he pointed. "Handgun. I know for a fact he's fantasized about it. Thought maybe today was going to be my lucky day. Been working on him for months now."

Nathalie shook her head. For a moment she had almost forgotten why she never saw her old friend anymore...

"When you fell you really didn't let the ground stop you, did you Jason?"

"You know, I thought about it long and hard and in the end I decided: better to be on the wrong side than on nobody's side."

He tried to laugh, but it sounded forced.

"And you know what? For her, it might even be better! You don't want to *know* what some of the others do to her..."

Nathalie had had enough of the conversation.

"Well, you should get used to being disappointed," she said. "You're not going to have any lucky day, not with this one."

Jason shrugged.

"Hey come on now," he said. "It's just a *job*,"

Nathalie smiled, and threw out her hands towards him. He just had time to understand what she was doing—he might not be an angel anymore but his eyes were still fast—before she made contact. His face had the barest second to register shock and fear, and then Jason shot backwards like a bullet. Angels can call on a supernatural strength if they require it, and nothing that is not divine can resist them.

She stood up and walked over to where Jason was frozen in mid air, caught by the sphere of timelessness along with the others. There might be more devils than angels, but thank goodness for where the advantages of strength lay. Jason had no more control now over the flow of time than a human would. But looking close, Nathalie was glad to see that he had employed one talent that still remained to him. Even in the small amount of time Jason had had at his disposal between her striking him and his body entering the sphere, he had been able to start dispersing his physical form. That was good, one less thing to worry about when she started the clock again.

She turned her attention back to the humans. The man looked intolerably smug, standing there so proud, adjusting his tie while the girl cowered amid the sheets. He had hurt her. She knew it, felt the pain as if she had been the one who had been hurt. He had hurt her before, and if nothing changed, he would hurt her again.

And he wasn't the worst one.

She was filled with rage at the whole wretched business. She had spent her whole existence travelling among the worst breeds of human sin, and knew how common it was. She had spent months, *years* sometimes on single assignments, carefully, patiently talking to people, giving them hope, shaking strength into the ones who thought themselves weak, and humility into the ones who thought themselves strong. And then someone like Jason would come along and with a little shove of will—or even a physical push, sometimes—would convince a doctor to murder his patients, or a priest to cheat on his vows. And she could do nothing, absolutely *nothing*. She could feel their pain, but never mend it. She could tell them not to kill, but not stop them pulling the trigger. Damn the Laws of Intervention! Damn them right to

Hell, and then maybe Hell would stop being so successful in invading the Earth!

She was so livid she did not know whether to weep or scream. Maybe…maybe it did not have to be that way.

The fire inside her had cooled a little; but something had melted in the heat, and now it was reforming in a different shape.

Perhaps she was not as impotent as she had thought. Perhaps she could help the girl—and the others—after all. Perhaps she could help all the others.

And maybe this one could still be saved. A starting point, at least. She found she wanted to try, just to spite Jason. He would not be getting this one for the fire.

She wondered how she would do it, and then decided that not intervening was not the same thing as being subtle, necessarily. She sauntered over to the man, and casually turned herself into a fiery conflagration with blistered flesh and scarred skin. Her eyes turned poisonous yellow with black cat-like slits instead of human pupils, and her hair flew up into a hissing, wailing mane of ash and smoke. With a gesture, she let time flow between them.

The man focussed on her, and his jaw dropped. He raised a hand to shield himself from the heat pouring off her.

"Repent! Repent!" shrieked Nathalie, who saw nothing wrong in resorting to drama, as long as it got the message across, and who anyway found she had grown rather tired of subtleties. "Thou art wicked! Thou art impure! Mend thy ways, O dog, lest my fate should befall you, too."

The man wailed and blubbered, and sank to the floor in abject terror.

"It is not yet too late for you, wicked sinner though you are!" she went on, embarrassed by how much she was enjoying herself. "You may yet save yourself!"

The man shook beneath her.

"How?" he screeched. "Please, how?"

"Discard your instrument of death, dog!" Nathalie cried. "Throw it under the bed, there,"

Shaking, the man rummaged desperately in his coat, pulled out the handgun, and flung it away as if it were a poisonous snake.

"Good!" screamed Nathalie. "I see you are not yet gone beyond reason! Now, will you repent of your sins and never come to this, or any place like it, again?"

The man nodded.

"And will you henceforth honor and love all humans as if they were your kin?"

"Yes! Yes!" screeched the man, shaking his head so vigorously that sweat flew from his brow.

"Then you may go!" Nathalie shouted, and slapped her hands together in a thunderclap explosion of sparks, just to emphasise her point.

Quick as a flash, the man picked himself up and scurried out of the room, whimpering like a scolded child.

"And call your mother more often," Nathalie called after him, just for good measure.

She sighed, and reassumed her normal form. The room darkened again.

Well, that was a start.

She looked at the girl, lying frozen on the bed.

She moved back into the dark of the room, and let herself blend into the shadows. Then she nodded, and allowed time to flow again. Jason unfroze and dissipated into a thousand wisps of smoke which burnt away on the instant, no doubt to reappear somewhere where he was not apt to be thrown through a wall.

Nathalie had Angel-senses, and a keen ability to detect the presence of mortal and immortal alike. Nevertheless, she was not infallible, and would have been surprised indeed if she had known how close Jason had chosen to transport himself.

«««—»»»

Rebecca awoke from cloying dreams and found she was alone. The man had gone. She started, and kicked herself out of the bed. She had not meant to fall asleep. Madam had found her asleep once before, and had beaten her so harshly that no man would come near her for a week. At first she hadn't been sure if it was a blessing or a curse. But then she realized it was definitely a curse, because Madam told her if she wasn't making money, she wasn't worth feeding, and starved her for five days straight. So now she strove to stay awake, and spent half her life tired. The only problem was, when it got to be time to sleep, more often than not she found she was not tired anymore. She just lay there, staring up at the cracks in the ceiling.

She pulled on her underwear and skirt, and hurried into her changing room—her *boudoir*, Madam called it, with a nasty smile on her lips—and began freshening her makeup. She worked as fast as she could, but she was only half done when she heard a knock on the door to her room, and a moment later the sound of hinges as someone creaked it open.

For a moment, her heart froze. Some of them, they didn't like it so much when she wasn't in the room ready and waiting for them, just waiting there on the bed for them the moment they came in. No, they didn't like that at all.

"'Becca?" came a voice, a little timid-sounding. "'Becca, are you there? It's me, Frank."

She let herself breathe out. It was Frank. He wasn't so bad, Frank, not so bad as far as her customers went. He never hit her, at least. As long as they didn't touch her face, Madam didn't mind the guys getting a little rough with her. Touching the face might slow down business. No, they didn't get to touch her face. Not unless they paid Madam extra.

Rebecca found that her hand was shaking. She had smudged her lipstick. She took a breath, and forced herself to be calm. Stop thinking, that was the trick. If you could stop thinking, then it was not so bad, not even the ones who wanted to pay extra.

Once you stopped thinking, it was not that big a step to stop the hurting, too.

"Be there in a minute, sweetie," she called out, rushing to finish her paint.

She finished shadowing her eyes, and was just about to head to the bedroom, when she felt…*odd*. There was a tingling all down her back. The hairs on her neck stood up, all together, and she suddenly knew someone was staring at her, standing right next to her and just staring right at her. She spun around, fists clenched to fight God-knows what. But the room was empty.

Frank called out for her. She shook herself. Maybe she was getting ill again. She hoped not. Madam didn't like it when the girls took ill.

Frank was waiting for her when she went into the bedroom. Still fully dressed. He was one who liked help with his clothes. Rebecca arranged a smile on her face, just as pretty as she could make it, and moved towards him.

But then the strangest thing happened. Just as she was leaning forward, just before she touched his shirt collar, she could have sworn the man…*flickered*. It was as if he'd moved slightly, just the tiniest bit, but all in an instant, like a fault on a videotape. She flinched back without meaning to, and started to laugh at her own surprise, but when she looked up to him to share the joke— Frank was one of those rare ones that she *could* have a joke with—she checked herself. Something was wrong with him. His eyes were too wide, and his mouth was ajar. And he was shaking.

"Frank?" she said. "Frank, you okay?"

His eyes swung towards her all of a sudden, as if someone had prodded him.

He swallowed, once, twice, three times.

Then he pulled out his wallet and emptied all his money onto the bed, quick as lightning. He even threw in the change from his pocket, and then—*chink*—his gold wristwatch, too, landed in the pile.

She stepped away from him then. Something was really *wrong* with Frank. His face was white. She wondered if he was having a stroke, she'd always wondered what that would look like.

For a moment she thought his eyes had glazed over, but then she realized he was looking over her shoulder. She fancied she

25

felt eyes on her back again, and she spun round. But no one was there. The room was empty apart from Frank and her.

When she turned back to Frank, he had tears in his eyes.

"I'm sorry, I'm so sorry," he said. "I'm…I didn't mean to… I, I'm sorry," he stammered.

And with that he left. He turned on his heel and practically ran for the door. She heard him clattering down the stairs, and then some other door further off slammed, and he was gone.

Rebecca looked at the money laid out on the bed, dumbfounded. It as much money as she had ever seen in her life. What should she do with it? Madam always handled the money. She would be angry if she found that Frank had given her some money. She wasn't allowed to keep money from the clients. No, the best thing she could do would be to scrape it all together into a pot or something and go right downstairs and give it straight to her. That way no one could say she was planning to keep the money, not any of it. She jumped to her feet. What would be best to put it in? How about an old makeup bottle? But they were all too small. After a thorough search she found a little plastic wallet in amongst her nylon stockings, and stuffed the money inside. She was just making for the door to take the money down to Madam, when she found herself thinking, *Why not wait until the end of the day? Madam's bound to be busy now. She'd much rather you waited until later.*

She paused at the door, confused. Now that she thought about it, it did seem that it would be a much better idea not to take the money to Madam right this instant. But she was sure there was some reason, some very good reason why she should…

No, she thought again, *Much better just to hide the purse for now, so that no one sees it, and then give it to Madam later. I'll just hide it for now, then I can neaten my makeup again before the next visitor arrives.*

She shook her head. Yes, that was right. She should just hide the money somewhere safe for now, and do her makeup.

She had plenty of time before anyone knocked on the door the next time, and was ready for them when they did. It was a stranger this time, not one of her regulars. But he had hardly walked in when the same thing happened. He flickered, just like Frank had done—and then all of a sudden he was throwing his money on the bed and apologising to her like a madman and then running out of the door so fast it was a wonder the carpet didn't catch fire.

And the same thing happened again, and again, and all the rest of the afternoon, until the light creeping in round the edges of the curtains was red and dusky, and in the darkness of the room Rebecca had to squint to see the notes as she stuffed them into the overflowing purse.

She didn't have a clue what was happening; and she didn't know whether to feel terrified or happy or bemused or all three rolled into one. But the fact that she was feeling *anything*, anything at all, was so unusual she could practically scream.

But she hadn't lost her senses so completely that she didn't notice the brisk footsteps outside the door. She had just enough time to wipe the smile from her face and shove the bulging purse under the bed, and then the door was flung open, and Madam strode in.

She wasn't alone. One of her regulars was with her, she recognized him even in the dim light seeping through the curtains.

It was Mr. Hyde.

"Rebecca, stand up," Madam commanded, and Rebecca found herself obeying the icy words before she could think. The habit was trained in deep.

The older lady slapped the wall with one gloved hand, and a bright white light sprung on overhead. Rebecca squinted. She felt that Madam could see right through her. She felt that the light was scolding her skin.

"Mr. Hyde has just come up to see you, and he tells me the door was locked," she went on, her voice not loud, but cold and hard as ice. "You know very well the rules do not permit the doors to be locked. I will not tolerate it, and I will make sure you understand me later tonight."

Tears sprung into Rebecca's eyes.

"I didn't lock the door," she stammered, half choking.

"What?" said Madam. "What did you say?"

"I didn't lock the door, *Madam*," she repeated. She didn't feel excited or bemused or happy anymore. Now she just felt dread. Desperate, she tried to claw at it, to force it back inside where it wouldn't hurt.

"How *dare* you talk back to me?" Madam hissed. "You will be silent! You will do as you are told!"

Rebecca swallowed, and stared at her feet.

Madam twisted like an eel and faced Mr. Hyde, and continued in quite a different tone of voice.

"I'm so sorry, Mr. Hyde," she said. "I don't know what has come over her. She is usually so very pliant."

"That's quite alright, pray don't mention it," growled Mr. Hyde from behind his grey moustache. "Perhaps I can teach the girl some manners."

It wasn't quite a question, but Rebecca understood what he meant well enough. So did Madam. She smiled and took the banknotes he held out to her, and she left the room.

"Well, well, well," Mr. Hyde chuckled to himself. Rebecca waited, staring at her feet, trying to control herself. She hadn't been ready for this. The others had put her off, the other men, they had put her off by the way they had acted. She had forgotten that there were men like Mr. Hyde, too.

You couldn't call him "Sweetie," like you could Frank.

Best not to say anything to him, if you could avoid it.

But Mr. Hyde just kept walking round the room, slow, steady, circling her, staring at her out of the corner of his eagle's eye.

He took his overcoat off, and hung it up on the back of the door.

"Well, well, well," he said again. He chuckled to himself.

Then he removed his expensive gloves and punched her in the face.

He was strong for such an old man, but Rebecca, stayed on her feet. She had been expecting it. Usually she would have started falling even before he touched her. It was easier that way.

But she felt something was different this time. Some part of her, some small part of her was saying, *no*. Not this time. She wouldn't fall over for him. She wouldn't fall over for this *bastard* again.

She wiped her mouth with the back of her hand and looked up at him. She met his eye. She caught it, just for a moment: surprise. Surprise and fear. And then it was gone, replaced by rage. But that moment was enough. That filled her with a savage joy, and as it rushed through her something broke. She wasn't powerless. She could make him angry. She could make him *afraid*.

He lunged at her. She didn't even bother trying to get out of the way. He hit her again. He held her and hit her. He kicked her and pulled her up and slapped her. He yanked her hair back and spat in her face and punched her again.

Then he threw her and she landed, dazed, half on the bed and half hanging off the edge.

He snorted and began to undress. Groggy, she looked up at him. His eyes roved over her body, seemed to suck up every inch of her. His lips glistened with spit; she could see his moist tongue trembling with excitement between the slight partings of his sharp teeth.

The purse, she thought, *Just grab the purse and go! I don't have to stay here!*

She grunted and half-rolled, half fell off the bed and onto the floor.

Behind her, she heard the sound of Mr. Hyde pulling his shoes off. She pulled the duvet away from the floor. There was the purse, of course, just where she'd left it.

But it wasn't alone.

There was a man underneath the bed.

She blinked. He was laying down flat, smoking a cigarette. He had sunglasses on, and a wicked smile, and he was holding a gun out to her.

"One of your clients dropped this," he offered, beaming at her.

He offered her the gun. She took it, and the man disappeared in a puff of cigarette smoke.

The Fall of the Angel Nathalie

Too dazed to wonder how crazy she must be to be hallucinating men under her bed, Rebecca raised herself unsteadily to her feet.

Mr. Hyde was naked now and moving towards her with a big grin on his wrinkled face.

He saw the gun in her hand. He stopped.

She was breathing hard. She kept having to wipe the blood from her eyes. He was standing between the door and her.

"Easy there, girl, easy there," said Mr. Hyde. "Just give me the gun now, we don't want this to get ugly,"

More ugly, you mean, she wanted to say, but her tongue was swollen, and she was breathing too hard to speak.

She groped for the purse under the bed without taking her eyes off Hyde. Something stung her hand, and she recoiled in pain. She glanced down, saw the purse, picked it up.

She began to edge around Hyde, making for the door.

"Just relax honey, there's a good girl," Hyde was saying. He was moving away from the door, but he kept his eyes fixed on her like a cat watching a mouse, as if he were waiting for her to make a mistake, waiting for her to remember how weak she was so he could end this ridiculous charade.

She reached the door, and twisted the handle. The latch clicked, and she eased the door open. She was free. All she had to do was run down the stairs and out the door. He couldn't stop her now. None of them could stop her now.

Not even Madam.

He lunged for her, grabbed her, threw her back into the room.

She didn't pull the trigger. Something in her was too deeply rooted.

She was still holding it when she hit the floor.

He advanced until he was standing over her. He grinned.

"Little girls shouldn't play with guns," he enunciated. He held his hand out for the weapon.

She moved forward like a trained dog to give it to him.

And then it was as if all the rage, all of the anger and hate and pain she had hidden within herself over the years was let loose, spilling out of her in one white-hot moment. Later, much later when she was an old woman, and was telling this story to her friends because it no longer mattered what anyone thought anymore, she would swear blind that she actually *felt* a hand brushing against her hair and into her skull, *felt* her anger being unlatched and allowed to course through her.

She fired the gun: once, twice and again.

Hyde staggered, surprised, disbelieving.

She pulled the trigger a fourth time. He fell.

She got up, and stood over him, and started kicking him. She didn't stop until her legs ached so much she could hardly move them.

She wondered why no one had come running as soon as they heard the first gunshot. She picked up the purse, and made for the door, dropping the gun by Hyde's body. She paused, returned, and flung open the curtains. Madam had always insisted that the curtains stayed closed.

It was beautiful outside, beautiful and still. There wasn't a sound at all, not a sound, and nothing was stirring there so much as an inch.

She gazed out for a minute, then turned and marched away without a backwards glance.

On her way down the stairs, Rebecca wondered at how quiet it was. Which was strange, because usually there were all kinds of noises coming from the various rooms. She got to the front hall, and started when she saw Madam—although she had already resolved that she would just walk by her, just walk straight on by the bitch, like she was sure she always could have done if she'd chosen to—but when she got closer, she saw that the older woman was asleep. Asleep standing up, leaning against a wall, her eyes half closed.

This was strange, but Rebecca barely gave it a moment's thought, because her body was screaming at her. How could she have not noticed such pain until now? Not that she minded—she would heal, and it was so much better to feel everything than nothing. But it was odd that what was hurting most of all was the mark on her arm. It looked like a cigarette burn.

She thought about the pain. She felt it. Somehow, that seemed to make it better. She opened the door and went out into the still night.

«««—»»»

Nathalie stood by the window and smoked the discarded cigarette right down to the filter. She waited until she had seen Rebecca turn the corner and head off out of her sight before relaxing the part of her mind that held the house timeless, and then exhaled a plume of blue smoke as the noise of life began to rise again from the rooms all around.

Well, that had not quite happened as she had intended. She had let herself get a little carried away. The money was one thing—a simple message delivered with fire-and-brimstone theatrics was nothing so out of the ordinary for her—but why on earth had she encouraged the girl to pull the trigger? She could have just let it be…

She made a face, and flicked the cigarette out into the night. But as it spun towards the earth, Jason materialized in mid-air and snatched it lazily from its flight, before disappearing and rematerializing again in the room next to her. He grinned from behind his sunglasses and used the glowing cigarette butt to light a fresh one he produced from inside his jacket pocket.

"Wow, you showed me," Jason drawled. "I mean, I thought I was good at leading these guys from the straight and narrow, but *you*…Bravo!"

He applauded her, a small waterfall of ash drifting from his cigarette with each clap.

"He would have killed her if she hadn't killed him," she rejoined, and almost succeeded in keeping the defensive tone from her voice.

"Absolutely. And she'd be sipping wine in the Garden right now, whilst he would have been one step further into our pockets. One big step."

Nathalie scowled at him, and yanked the cigarette from his unresisting hand.

32

"She deserved more of a life than that before the Garden," she muttered, inhaling deep into her lungs. "And he'd walked the earth quite long enough. He won't be missed."

"Well said!" Jason exclaimed. "I certainly had no further use for the man. He's been ours for the last twenty years, anyway. No sense keeping him hanging round here any longer, just waiting for some serendipitous act of redemption to put all our hard work to ruin. No, from our point of view he's much better harvested while ripe. And it frees us up to work on some new client. Take a lovely girl for instance, her whole existence spent enduring the ills of evil humans, never hurting a fly despite the pain life has dealt her. Why, how much more satisfying to claim this girl with one terrible temptation than to gently lead a thousand sinners down a path they've already set themselves on!"

Nathalie managed a bitter smile at that.

"I've looked into that girl's heart," she said. "You think I would have pushed her to shoot him if I thought that would send her to you? There's pain; and that will be with her always. And anger; and she will have to fight to control that, now that it's been released. But there's nothing broken in her. No twists or knots or perversions which could condemn her to your workshops. You shan't have her."

At this, Jason quite lost control of himself, and roaring with laughter, flung himself to the ground and pounded the soles of his feet on the wooden floorboards.

"Oh, priceless, my dear, priceless!" he managed to choke out. He pulled off his sunglasses, and looked up at her with his yellow Daemon's eyes. "Whatever made you think I was talking about her?"

«««—»»»

Nathalie realized that the air had grown very still. The sounds coming from elsewhere in the building had stopped completely. It was as if some vast clockwork wheel that had spun since the beginning of forever had snapped at last, and the world itself had ceased to turn. The only noise came from Jason as he giggled and snorted on the floor by her feet.

She swallowed.

He tricked me, she thought, *He knew I couldn't stand to see her killed. He put the gun into her hand. He made me commit Intervention.*

She was too numb to be angry.

"Oh, I didn't trick you—I *tempted* you," said Jason, as if he could read her thoughts. "That's the whole point with *temptation*. Free will. You of all people should know that. I didn't *make* you do anything."

"I didn't do anything wrong," Nathalie said, but her voice sounded weak in her own ears.

"Oh, stop it," Jason muttered. "Such tremendous bouts of cliché."

He sat up straight and stared at her plaintively.

"If you only knew how many times we poor Daemons have to endure that wretched line from our clients…I must say, it hurts to hear it coming from you, a verified Angel!"

Nathalie opened her mouth to speak again, but then she noticed the shadows. They were shedding away from everything, from the corners of the room, from the darkness around the bed and the edges of the walls; they were massing together, turning and writhing, folding in on themselves and becoming blacker than the night outside.

It's coming, she thought. *Aekmar was right.*

Jason looked at her, serious for once. Nathalie wasn't sure, but she thought she saw something in his eyes, something of their old friendship.

"Don't run." he admonished her, a sad half-smile on his lips. "It is faster than you. It is stronger than you. It will claim you. Don't run like I did. Face it with dignity."

Nathalie just looked at him. Hurt and betrayal twisted within her.

She wanted to say something, to ask him how he could have willed for this to happen. But there was nothing to be said. She turned back to the shadows.

34

They were mounting one another now; and rising together out of the ground, they flowed outwards to form a shape which flickered and shifted as shadows do in the twilight places were neither light nor darkness is master. They formed something at once vast and gaunt, imposing and ephemeral, tall as a spire yet shrunk to within the confines of the room.

The Hecatomb had come.

Nathalie felt her legs go limp. They could barely support even her slight frame. The thing before her was more terrible than she ever could have imagined, and it seemed to suck from her every ounce of strength.

It came towards her, and as it did so, the circumference of her world pulled in around her, until nothing else existed but her and the shadows that walked to her side with a deadly grace.

This was real. This was happening to her.

She could not make herself believe it.

The Hecatomb was before her, the most terrible of Angels, the Angel of Shadows. It had come for her, and she would submit to its judgement.

It loomed closer, and yet she could not discern any feature amidst the shifting darkness.

And with a jolt she realized she could not stand limp and meek before her own demise. She would not be lost without a struggle. In that moment, all the strength returned to her limbs. Life flowed into her again, pumping with the blood in her veins, and with a wordless cry she launched herself towards the window. With a single blow she tore through the bricks and glass and metal, and sailed out into the night, fragments of the wall trailing in lazy arcs behind her. The ground loomed up to meet her, but then—*snap!*—her her wings unfolded with a flourish, her beautiful ruby wings, soft as feathers, hard as gemstones, light as light itself. She worked them with all her strength, and soared up into the sky. The ground vanished beneath her beating wings, and clouds surrounded her. But soon she was above the clouds, too, and sailing very high up beneath the stars. Then she felt a moment of triumph. Her heart rose up inside her chest, and its *thump, thump, thump* was like the singing of a hundred nightingales in spring.

But not for long.

The Hecatomb was with her.

It was beside her, she saw, keeping her pace with ease, a darker shadow in the dark of night.

Frantic to escape, she beat her wings: up and up she rocketed, until the air became too thin, and she realized that she could go no more. Tears welled in her eyes; but they froze as soon as they left her face, and fell as crystals back towards the earth, many, many miles far below.

Now she understood that she was lost. She could not fight the Hecatomb. She was weaker, she was slower, she was powerless before the Angel of Shadows.

So she stopped striving. She folded her wings and closed her eyes, and let herself fall.

But she did not fall far, not yet.

She was held fast. She opened her eyes, and there it was before her: the Hecatomb. It embraced her, sliding shadows about her waist and—to her surprise—with unspeakable tenderness through her hair and across her frozen cheeks. And now she could see its face, and she was stunned, because she perceived that it had no terrible visage of teeth or snarls; but rather one of tenderness, and of beauty.

It whispered in her ears, words that she could not catch, and yet their meaning was plain. They were the words spoken to calm an animal that knows it is near to death. She felt her heart beat slowing. She was still scared, terrified. But she was no longer wild with the fear. She understood now.

She took a deep breath, flexed her beautiful wings one last time, and looked up into the Hecatomb's diamond icicle eyes.

The Hecatomb smiled at her, once, with sadness.

Then it reached behind her with its shadowed limbs, and severed her ruby wings from her alabaster back.

PART TWO

There was a city, and in that city there was a street. In the street was a car, and in the car was a small body, very thin and miserable, curled up in the back seat.

There were lots of back streets in that city, and this street was one of those. It lead from nowhere into nowhere, between two nowhere districts, and it was always lonely. It was the kind of place where you could be all alone even when you were surrounded by people, the kind of place where no one said "hello" and everyone kept their eyes on the ground.

The car hadn't moved for months. No one knew anymore to whom it belonged, and no one cared, either. The street was deserted, except for the girl in the back seat.

The girl curled up in the back seat wasn't crying, but that was only because she wasn't the type of girl who cried. She popped the top off another bottle of pills and emptied as many as she could into her mouth. A few spilled out and came to rest amongst the filthy contents of the floor. The girl ignored them. She unscrewed the bottle of vodka and took a deep pull. She gagged briefly but forced herself to swallow. Most of the pills stayed down.

She looked about briefly. Her eyes were red and covered in watery films; it was difficult to drink vodka straight.

In the distance, someone she didn't know shouted something, but no one answered.

It was funny to be seeing all this for the last time, she thought. It was all so familiar.

She knew every inch of this neighbourhood, every broken window and chipped paving stone. It felt so good to be leaving it all behind.

I wonder how long it will be before someone finds me, she thought.

Will it be Max?

Maybe he'll be taking King for a walk. Maybe King will get a whiff of something, come to investigate. She could imagine the dog's little black nose twitching in the chill February air, could see the frown on Max's face as he peered in through the dusky glass windows, tried to make sense of the shape curled up in the darkness.

She hoped it wouldn't be Max. Max would clear things up, make sure Suzanne didn't see her.

She wanted Suzanne to see her. She wanted Suzanne to see what she had done.

Maybe King will eat me, she thought.

Maybe King will eat me all up until nothing is left, and no one will even realise I'm gone.

Not Max, not Suzanne, not anyone.

She coughed and shook her head. Her thoughts were getting fuzzy round the edges.

Something was whistling, far off. Someone shouted out again, and the echoes danced around the empty streets.

Maybe Will could find me, she thought; and then she remembered what had happened to Will, and why, and all at once she was reaching for the vodka bottle again, pulling back on it until nothing was left, not a drop, and her whole body felt on fire.

She slid the bottle out through the opening at the top of the car window, and it smashed loudly on the pavement.

When the tinkling died down, she realized the whistling sound was still there. It was getting louder.

She raised her head from the seat, tried to figure out where it was coming from.

Was someone out there? Was someone watching her?

She tried to call out, but her mouth wouldn't work properly. She slumped against the window, peered into the desolate, run-down street, tried to get a view of what was making the noise.

Her heart was thumping fast in her chest. It felt like it kept skipping beats, and her breath wouldn't come properly.

She didn't want to be in the car anymore. Something felt wrong, something felt heavy.

The whistling got louder.

She scratched at the car door, lunging for the handle. Her arms felt too big. The tips of her fingers had gone numb.

Somehow she managed to unlock the rusty door. It swung open and she half-fell out into the street, discarded pills and empty bottles rattling out by her side.

She didn't know what she was doing; she just knew she couldn't stay in the car. Something sharp bit into her arm. It was a piece of the broken vodka bottle.

I'm going to die soon, she thought.

I don't want to die in a car, not in that old rusty junk car.

I want to die in the open air.

She staggered across to a doorway opposite, collapsed down and looked around.

The whistling was so loud now, she almost couldn't hear herself breathe.

Where was it coming fro…?

She heard the noise of the impact almost before she saw the body flash in front of her.

It dropped out of the sky and slammed into the car.

All the windows smashed at once, and one of the front tyres shot off faster than the eye could follow. The noise was deafening.

The car folded into two around the body and bounced back

up into the air. It rose higher than a bus, twisted on its side, and fell again, thudding into the ground so hard the pavement shook.

A rain of small fragments of metal and glass and plastic pattered down around her. A hubcap spun on the spot, stopped, toppled. There was a moment of silence.

The girl looked at the car, what was left of it. She struggled up to her feet and staggered over to look at the sad remains of wrecked machinery. The whistling noise had stopped. In the distance, what sounded like a thousand car alarms were suddenly going off.

Something glistened wetly. Something was folded up in the metal remains of the car.

She moved closer. Her stomach heaved. Desperately, she tried to force the vomit down.

No, she thought.

Today is the day I die.

Don't be sick.

She looked closer.

It was a woman. A woman was wrapped up in the metal corpse of the old car.

She was slender and naked and covered in blood.

Her dark hair was matted with blood and stuck to two gaping scars on her back, just beneath her shoulder blades.

Something drifted down out of the grey sky, and grazed gently against the girl's cheek. She ignored it. She couldn't take her eyes off the woman.

As she watched, the woman's shoulder blades shuddered, and two cracked shafts of bone twitched upwards forlornly out of the woman's back. More soft somethings fell slowly by her face, unnoticed.

The girl's stomach knotted.

She tried to keep it in, but she couldn't.

She wanted to keep it in, the vodka and the pills, wanted more than anything to close her eyes and drift away.

But the bones were so broken, and the blood was so blossomed, and there was something unbearable about the abandonment of those bare white shoulders.

40

Laura vomited up her death into the coldness of the street, while ruby red feathers drifted down out of the sky around her. This day wasn't her day to die, after all.

«« —— »»

No one noticed Laura when she hurried back to her mother's flat to get the blanket, just as no one had noticed her leave that morning, just as no one had noticed the absence of the vodka bottle or the ransacking of the medicine cabinet. Her family wasn't the sort of family that noticed things.

Which was exactly why what had happened to Will, had happened to Will...

No. She pushed the thought away. She couldn't think of him.

Back in the street, everything was as she had left it. Not a soul had come to investigate the noise. Not a soul had seen it but her.

The woman still lay in the broken hulk of the old car. Blood and oil were pooling together in a little hollow under the shattered bodywork, trickling out in little twists and being washed away by the rain.

Laura stepped forward, hesitated. Now that it came to it, she was reluctant to touch the woman.

What if she had broken her neck? Wouldn't it be better to keep her still?

Why not just call an ambulance and get back to the business of killing herself? This wasn't her problem. She had a lot of problems, but this one wasn't hers.

But something told her that would not do.

The woman had fallen out of the sky, she had torn a car in half in her descent—and survived, somehow—and those wounds on her back...

A hospital wouldn't help this woman.

Maybe Laura could, though...

Maybe she could help someone, at least...

"Hey, lady," she tried. Her voice sounded thin and useless.

The woman stirred but didn't move.

Laura moved closer and draped the blanket over her narrow shoulders. Wetness soaked through the cloth and stuck the blanket to her skin.

The woman shifted and cried out. She lashed backwards with one of her arms, and Laura only just darted her head back in time to avoid getting a slap in the face.

"Hey, take it easy," she said. "It's just a blanket. I'm just trying to get you covered up."

The woman had slumped again. She was breathing hard now, though. She coughed.

"What…where am I?"

"You're out East," said Laura. "You demolished a car. Don't worry, no one's gonna mind. Maybe no one's even gonna notice," she added to herself.

"That's not what I mean. Which continent? Which city?"

Laura snorted.

"Er, London. Europe," she said.

"I thought so," the woman replied. She paused. "This hurts," she added. "A lot."

"I'm not surprised," replied Laura. "Have you broken anything? Can you walk?"

The woman shook her head.

"Nothing's broken," she said. "Everything's wrong, but nothing's broken."

She pulled one leg up under her and staggered unsteadily to her feet. She tried to catch her balance, failed, and went reeling backwards into Laura.

"Hey, not so fast! Take it easy!"

Laura managed to keep them both standing. The woman shifted awkwardly. The blanket was draped over her shoulders. It left most of her body naked, covered in blood and dirt, but she didn't seem to care.

Laura hastily caught the blanket and wrapped it round the woman, covering her up.

"Thank you," the woman muttered, and it was only then that Laura noticed her eyes.

They were huge and yellow as poison. They were slitted vertically, like a cat's.

"What the hell are you?" Laura asked.

The woman smiled. Her teeth looked very sharp.

"You know, I've been asking myself that for the last three days, all the time I've been falling," she said. "And I think the answer is: something else."

Laura looked at her uncertainly for a moment.

Suddenly, she found that she was smiling too, for the first time in what felt like forever.

"I've felt like I was something else before, too," she said. "It's nice not to be the only one."

The woman extended a slender hand. Somehow, it suddenly looked completely clean.

"My name is Nathalie," she said.

That was how things began.

《《—》》

"So you're a fallen angel?" said Blake suspiciously. He turned his marshmallow above the fire and cursed as half of it slid off the fork and into the flames.

They were sitting in a little ring around the barbecue, Nathalie, Laura and Blake. Blake was Laura's oldest friend. When Will had been taken to the hospital, it was Blake who stayed up with Laura and talked things through. When Laura had cursed and raged, and wanted nothing so much as to go to her mother and do…certain things…it had been Blake who had talked her down.

It was Blake's place they were at now.

"I don't like the term 'fallen angel'," said Nathalie, fishing the marshmallow out from the fire with her fingers and popping it into her mouth. "I prefer to think of myself as an angel who no longer works for the Establishment."

"And what does an angel do, anyway?"

Laura shook her head. She had grown up with Blake, and she loved him, but he *was* a bit slow sometimes.

"They help people, you idiot!" she glowered at him. "You know, 'angel'? As in, 'guardian angel'?"

"Oh, right, yeah," said Blake, absent-mindedly skewering another marshmallow. "So who did you guard then?"

"Oh, whoever I wanted," said Nathalie. "There was never a lack of clients."

"So, you're sort of a general freelance angel with a special interest in helping people, right?" Blake frowned with concentration as he tried to get his marshmallow crisp but not molten.

"Yes; yes, you could say I intend to go freelance," agreed Nathalie.

"You mean you haven't started yet?" asked Laura.

"Of course I've started!" said Nathalie. "You're here, aren't you?"

"Wait a minute, *I* was the one who came to help *you*!" complained Laura.

"That's true. But you were also the one who would have died if you didn't have someone to help. I saved you just as surely as if I'd pumped your stomach myself."

"What's she talking about, Laura?" asked Blake, but no one answered, and the silence stretched on into the night.

"What do you do, Blake?" asked Nathalie at length.

Blake shrugged.

"Nothing much," he said. "Go to college. Gonna try and get an apprenticeship in September. Nothing as interesting as being an angel."

Nathalie nodded.

"Do you want to come and work for me?" she said.

"What?" said Blake, at the same time as Laura said, "Him? What about me?"

"Both of you, I mean," said Nathalie. "I want you both to come and work for me. You can be my assistants."

Blake frowned.

"I'm not sure about that," he said. "What are the hours like?"

"Erratic," said Nathalie. "But the pay's good. And you get to do something meaningful with your life."

A thin drizzle of rain began to fall.

Nathalie clicked her fingers and the fire leapt up. Raindrops fizzled and spat above them, completely failing to reach their heads.

"Also, you get to see lots of cool things like that," said Nathalie.

Blake nodded.

"OK," he said. "I'm in."

"Good," said Nathalie, getting to her feet. "Be ready. I'll be back soon."

She walked away into the night, and suddenly it was just the two of them, getting wet in the February drizzle.

«« — »»

That night, next to each other in the darkness, Blake tried to ask her about what she had done—what she had tried to do—that morning.

"I don't want to talk about it," she said, which was nearly true.

"What about me?" he said at last.

She shrugged.

"It's not about you. It's about me."

"You think I'd be able to just go on like nothing had happened if I woke up one day and found you'd topped yourself?" he asked her.

She smiled, because that was exactly what Blake would do.

"You accept things," she told him. "You accepted that I needed you when Will…when all the stuff with Will happened. You accepted it when I told you the woman I brought with me had fallen out of the sky because she was an angel who'd just had her wings cut off. That's you."

He laid a hand gently on her leg. Her eyes widened slightly.

"And you'll accept it now when I tell you—again—that the other time was just a one off, and that we're just good friends."

"I'd accept it better if it came with exceptions…?" he tried hopefully.

THE FALL OF THE ANGEL NATHALIE

There was a cold silence.

His hand moved away, and she relaxed.

"I'll accept it. I don't have to like it." His voice was forlorn.

"I'll accept that as an apology. And you'll accept this as 'goodnight'."

«««—»»»

"I circled the Earth three times as I fell, such was the height from which I was dropped," said Nathalie.

The priest looked at her levelly. He tried not to yawn. It never went down well to yawn at the crazies, even when they woke you up at 3am and demanded they talk with you in a sanctified space. This one seemed especially unsettled. Who in their right mind wore sunglasses in the middle of the night?

He had lived in the little house next to the church for twenty years, and the inconvenience of the occasional midnight confession was more than compensated for by the financial aspects of this arrangement.

Still, it could get somewhat tiresome.

"I see, my child," he said, pinching his thigh to try and stay awake. "That must have been rather terrifying."

"Actually, no," said Nathalie, brightly. "Well, the first hour or so was pretty unpleasant. I'd been used to flying, you see, not falling. Falling was different. Much more of a one-direction-only sort of a thing. I did a lot of screaming in that first hour. But it's amazing the things you can grow bored with. And the pain...I got used to the pain, too.

"It was like...can you imagine someone taking a knife, an impossibly sharp, diamond-edged knife, and running it over your arms? Not actually touching them, you understand. Just running the blade near.

"Only, you suddenly realized this knife was so...sharp...it had cut through your arms entirely. You didn't even notice it. And the pain was only there when you thought about it. You kept on forgetting they were gone. That's what it was like. I

46

kept on forgetting. I kept on not believing it. I'd try to move them, and it would just sting slightly, here, just under my shoulder. And I would still be falling. And I would still be bleeding."

The priest frowned. He had thought, once, several years ago about getting a panic button fitted somewhere in the church, maybe under the altar, or somewhere in the confessional. In the light of day, of course, such ideas had seemed perfectly barmy, but there were times…

"And why was it you were, ahem, cast out, as it were, my child?" he asked.

"Oh, that's the worst thing about it!" exclaimed Nathalie. "I got tempted—by another ex-angel, incidentally—into Intervening in the life of a young woman. I influenced her, released all the anger she had buried inside of her, so that she had the power to kill the man who was about to kill her."

"That hardly seems fair," said the priest, interested despite himself. "I mean, surely if she did it in self defence…remember my child, God is forgiveness."

Nathalie held her arms up.

"Hey, I don't make the rules up!" she said. "But I agree. It does seem a bit harsh. Three thousand years of loyal service, one cock-up and suddenly I'm out on my ear. Thanks a lot, God!"

"You're three thousand years old?" said the priest, impressed.

"I know," Nathalie flashed him a smile. "I don't look a day older than twenty five, right? I still get I.D.'d buying cigarettes sometimes."

The priest steepled his fingers. At least this one was a little unusual, he had to admit.

"I must say, after all this, I would have thought you'd be more…well, upset," he said.

"I'll be honest with you, for the first two days I was pretty pissed off," said Nathalie. "But you get a lot of time to think. When you're falling. Once you get used to it.

"And I began to think…maybe I'm better off without my wings. Maybe that's why this was allowed to happen. Maybe they wanted an agent who could work outside of the laws of Intervention. Maybe I was *supposed* to get cut. Maybe it's all part of the Plan."

She sighed.

"And then I thought: there is no Plan. Not even a plan with a little 'p'.

"There's just people trying to do good things, and people trying to mess things up.

"What kind of a God would go to all this trouble of making laws of Intervention—and enforcing them with something as awful as the Angel of Shadows, the one who clipped me—what kind of a God would go to those kind of lengths, and then sneakily double-bluff one of their own into breaking them?

"Not a God I'd want to be working for. Which is why I don't work for the Establishment any more. And I'll tell you now, I'm very excited about what's ahead of me. I think I'm going to make some real progress.

"Just you wait. Watch this space. You'll see. I just wanted people to know that."

Nathalie stood up and stretched.

"Well Father, thanks for listening," she said.

"You are welcome, my daughter," replied the priest, rising too, and walking her back down the vestibule. "But one question: why did you come *here* to tell me that? God is in all things and all places, you know."

Nathalie laughed.

"Oh, Father," she smiled. "I wasn't coming here to tell God! God probably knows all about it, but whatever God is, just because it's listening doesn't mean it cares.

"I came here to speak because I wanted someone to talk to, and priests who have been woken in the dead of night are good listeners. Or good at pretending to listen."

And also, she added to herself, because creatures other than men listen at the threshold places.

She thought it only fair to warn them before she began.

«‹‹—›»»

Nathalie came and collected them three days later, and took them to a small flat above a newsagents in Dulwich.

"It's not much, but we need an office to operate from," she told them. She didn't say how she had come by the flat, but there was a strange smell that clung to the curtains, and a few suspicious stains on the floor. Their neighbors didn't meet their eyes, and gave them a wide berth.

Laura did not say goodbye to her mother or to Max. She rubbed King's head and whispered something in his ear. She wondered how long it would be before anyone realized she was gone.

"What exactly do you want us to do?" Blake wanted to know.

"Oh, you know. Assisting. Helping out," said Nathalie, vaguely.

"I'm still not sure I quite get what it is you do," said Blake. "How can I help you when I don't know what you even do?"

Laura rolled her eyes.

"Just make the tea and deal with the paperwork, then," she told him.

But Nathalie said they should both come with her when she went to see her first client. She wanted them to see how it was done.

"Who's your first client, then?" asked Laura.

"I don't know," she told them. "But don't worry, we won't have to wait long."

She was right, of course.

«‹‹—›»»

"That one beats his wife," said Nathalie, and threw some bread into the water.

A clutch of ducks swarmed over and began splashing furiously for the food.

"What, that one there?" asked Laura. "The one with the white hair and the glasses? Really?"

Nathalie nodded.

"Not as much as he used to. He still does it, though."

"Doesn't look the type," said Blake, shaking his head.

Nathalie gave him a half smile.

"Are you calling me a liar?" she asked him.

Blake shrugged.

"Just saying you might be wrong," he said.

"Shut up, you idiot!" said Laura.

"No, it's a fair point," said Nathalie. "You don't know if I'm any good at this yet. Why don't you go and ask him?"

The two women looked at Blake. He glanced from one to the other.

"Alright, then, I will."

Blake got up and put his gloves in his pockets.

Nathalie and Laura watched as he walked over to the white-haired man.

"I'll say this for him: he's not a coward," commented Laura. She paused. "Maybe he's too stupid to be a coward." she added.

Blake walked back over, holding his eye.

"I think you were probably right, Nathalie," he said. "He's stronger than he looks, too."

"So is he going to be your first client?" asked Laura, but Nathalie shook her head.

"No-o," she said. "Hopefully Blake asking him will have done some good. And you can't spread yourself too thin. There's a lot worse than him about. You have to be a bit selective."

They looked around the park.

"What about him?" asked Blake.

"Nothing worth mentioning," said Nathalie.

"Her?" said Laura.

"She drowned a cat once. It was a long time ago, though."

"How about that one?" Blake nodded with his head.

Nathalie wrinkled her nose.

"Well, it's not exactly nice, but it doesn't quite deserve an Intervention," she said. "Anyway, I think the dog quite likes it."

Blake and Laura pondered this information in silence.

"Aha," said Nathalie, her eyes narrowing

"What?" said Laura.

"I think we have something worth working on," said Nathalie. She looked almost eager.

The others followed her gaze as she watched a thin woman in a white jogging trousers do stretches a little way off by the flower beds.

"What does she do?" asked Blake, but Nathalie just shook her head.

"Oh, you'll see," she said.

They waited until the woman left the park, and followed her at a discrete distance.

«««—»»»

Blake complained when they got onto the bus.

"Angels don't have to use public transport, do they?" he wanted to know.

He smiled and looked at Laura, but Laura did not smile back.

She had seen where the bus was going.

"I told you, I'm not an angel anymore," Nathalie reminded him. "We go on the bus because she's about to get on, too."

They had left the park before Nathalie's chosen woman had finished her stretches, but Nathalie knew all about her, it seemed, and at which bus stop to wait .

The bus lurched off. Three stops later, the woman boarded. She sat down a few seats ahead of them. If she recognized them from the park, she gave no sign of it.

Blake looked at her uniform in some surprise.

"She's a nurse," he whispered to Laura, and then. "Oh," he said.

"Yes, we're going to the hospital," Nathalie told them.

She looked at Laura. Laura tried not to meet her eyes, but there was some strength there that made her turn her head.

"We are not going there to see your brother, Laura," Nathalie said, softly.

Laura shook her head.

"He's not my brother anymore," she said. "I'm not sure what he is now, but he's not my brother."

"We don't have to go, Laura," said Blake, but Laura shrugged.

"Why should I care?" she told them, and they spent the rest of the journey in silence.

«««—»»»

Marie smiled a normal smile as she walked onto the ward, and everyone she saw smiled back. Why not? Marie was popular. Everyone loved Marie. The other nurses, the doctors, the parents, the children.

She was young and pretty. She had red hair—dyed red—that made the children think she was fun, even when they were about to go for an operation, and she had a full, throaty laugh and told stories that were not quite decent. How could they not love her?

The ward smelt of disinfectant and hospital food and sickness. She put her bag away and began getting on with the tasks of the day. It was a good job, but everyone was always so busy.

That would make it easier, she thought.

People who were busy didn't have time to notice everything.

At 6:00pm, she handed over a few little jobs to another nurse, and went for her break. She sat in the tea room and chatted in a perfunctory sort of a way with two doctors; in her head, she went over the details one last time.

As she was leaving the room, for just one moment there was a strange flickering in one corner of her eye, and she almost jumped out of her skin because she had the sudden impression that three people had abruptly flashed out of nowhere and were standing very close to her, looking at her, watching what she did.

The flickering passed. She put it down to stress. She might look normal, but that was taking an awful lot of effort. Inside, she felt like she might die. Her heart was hammering like crazy and her mouth was very dry.

She went back to the ward. It was emptier now. Some of the staff had gone home, but those who were left were still busy.

And then it was time to do the drug round, and then it was time to welcome a new patient to the ward, and then it was just time.

Time to act.

She smiled at the other nurse, said she was going to the toilet, and went instead to the neonatal unit on the floor above. Her identity card made the little red light turn green; the door buzzed and let her in.

There he was, as beautiful as when she had last seen him two nights ago.

He was very healthy. He didn't really need to still be in hospital, but the consultant was being cautious.

His mother came to visit every day, of course.

Marie would never have left.

His mother was a very impressive woman. She was very busy. She had a successful business and three other children to take care of, not to mention a new boyfriend whom she had missed a lot during her pregnancy.

Marie was an impressive woman in her own way, too, but she did not have a business, or a boyfriend, or any children.

She would never have any children. Not any of her own.

She would never be pregnant, never find out what morning sickness was really like, never waddle to the toilet thirty times in one day, or enjoy eating for two, or struggle to get the weight off again afterwards.

When she had been a child herself, Marie had got sick. She had to have several operations. She survived, of course, but not intact.

It wasn't fair, Marie thought.

She loved children, loved them so much.

It wasn't fair that she would never have one of her own.

But then, it didn't *have* to be that way, did it...?

The door beeped again, and let Marie back out into the corridor.

She held him close to her. His little body felt so warm; it was a precious thing.

THE FALL OF THE ANGEL NATHALIE

No one stopped her as she left the building. The wind outside felt cold and free. She would get in a taxi and they would go as far away as they could. She had it all arranged. She had money, passports with false names, aeroplane tickets and boat tickets and hotel reservations, and a new job, thousands of miles from here, in a distant country.

She walked towards the taxi rank. Something flickered as her hand touched the handle, and in one instant she saw it all.

She saw them fleeing across the country, getting to the airport, boarding the plane. She saw the news reports and the headlines in the tabloids. She saw the tears on his mother's face, saw the steel in her eyes. She saw the plane land, she saw the police waiting for them. She saw the jail cell and how many years it stretched on for. She saw the disgust in the faces of all her friends, all at once and forever. She saw the little baby and the boy he would become and the teenager and the adult and the old man after, and each version of him had something broken inside, and each version of him knew whose fault that was, too. She saw, at last, her own death, not an old woman, but a fractured one; and she was so glad for it when it came that she wept and wept and wept, and only realized she was still holding the baby in her arms when the taxi driver came round to where she had slumped outside the passenger side door and said words to her that she didn't start to understand until he had repeated them several times. She looked at him blankly as he helped her to her feet; then she turned and told him, "thank you," and turned away before she started crying again.

No one stopped her on her way back into the hospital. After she had put him back in his crib, she felt so light she cried more tears, but these were happy ones, and after that she always believed passionately in second chances.

One of the other nurses commented on her red eyes, but they matched her red hair and her smile, and no one thought twice about it when she told them she had hay fever, because even though it was February, something flickered when she said it, and the room was full of peace.

«««—»»»

"Go on then, what else can you do?" challenged Blake.

He knocked back his whisky, and poured himself another.

Nathalie took a long pull on the cigarette she was smoking and blew the smoke out of the open window. The sounds of Dulwich on a dreary Tuesday night drifted up in exchange.

"Well, I can burn things, obviously," said Nathalie.

"Boring!" said Blake, at the same time as Laura said, "Seen it! Next!"

"Um, well, I can look into people and see everything about them. See what they want, what makes them tick. See what horrible things they might do." She flicked her cigarette butt out of the window and poured herself a whisky.

"We know all about that!" complained Laura. "We've seen it! And how you can make people think things. Like, make them think we're not there, make them think they're seeing into the future, etcetera etcetera."

Nathalie swilled the whisky round her mouth and looked thoughtful.

"Well…" she said. "I'm really strong as well. I mean physically. I'm hard as nails."

There was a pause.

"You don't *look* so strong," said Blake.

There was another silence.

"I bet *I'm* stronger than you," said Blake.

Laura rolled her eyes.

"I bet you couldn't knock me over," said Blake.

Nathalie poured the rest of the whisky into her mouth, swallowed, and sighed.

"OK, then," she said.

Blake grinned. He stood up and pulled his T-shirt up over his head.

"Right," he said, "here's how it works. I stand here. You stand over there. You punch me once in the belly—you're not allowed a run-up. If I fall over, you win. If I go down, you win."

"And the loser has to drink!" added Laura.

"Right, and the loser has to drink," repeated Blake, absent-mindedly drinking his drink and burping loudly.

"Fine," said Nathalie. "But you hit me first."

Blake looked at her sideways.

"No," he said. "I don't hit women."

"I'm not a woman," said Nathalie. "Remember? I'm something else."

Blake looked from Nathalie to Laura, then shrugged.

"You're the boss," he said. "But promise me you won't get angry and set me on fire."

Nathalie nodded and got to her feet, only staggering slightly.

"I would *never* set you on fire," she said. "I promise."

She was wearing a white vest and black jeans. She pulled the vest up. Her abdomen was slender and pale.

"Go on," she said. "As hard as you can."

Blake pulled his fist back.

He looked at Nathalie. She smiled and gave him a wink.

He hit her.

There was a nasty cracking noise. Her body stayed absolutely still.

"Ow," said Blake. "What are you *made* of?"

"Not sure," said Nathalie. "The same stuff as seraphim and goblins, I think; but baked longer. There isn't a word for it. My turn."

Blake looked somewhat less confident.

"You can back down if you want?" suggested Nathalie.

Blake shook his head.

"No way," he said. "I'm not scared of you. Well, not very much scared of you."

He pulled up his shirt, let it drop, drank some whisky out of the bottle, pulled his shirt up again, and screwed his eyes shut.

"Go on then," he said. "Quick, before I sober up."

Nathalie flashed Laura a grin, turned, and slapped Blake on the belly.

There was a crashing noise as Blake flew through the air and landed on a table, which promptly disintegrated beneath him into a collection of wooden shards and bent screws.

Everyone burst out laughing, even Blake.

They found it so funny, it took them a few moments to realise there were four people laughing, not three.

"Aren't you going to introduce me to your friends?" said the man with dark hair. He was slender and quite good looking. He wore a sharp black suit and sunglasses. He smiled like a shark.

Nathalie sighed.

"Laura, Blake, this is Jason. Jason is an old…" she let her shoulder slump. "Well, he's an old something."

"Charmed," said Jason, kissing Laura's hand, and helping Blake up from the wreckage of the table.

Nathalie looked at him. He hadn't changed.

She had, though…

She slapped him, hard, around the face.

It sounded like a slab of meat being slammed against a table.

"That's for tricking me," she said.

Jason gave her a reproachful look and felt his cheek with one hand.

"I told you, I didn't *trick* you, I *tempted* you," he said. "That's what I do. You can't hold it against me for following my nature. That would be, well, unnatural."

Nathalie snorted.

"Don't try and hide behind your 'nature'," she told him. "My wings are cut now, too, remember? You don't see me suddenly giving up the cause, do you? You are responsible for your actions, just as I am for mine."

"What's he on about?" asked Laura.

"It was Jason who arranged for me to Fall," said Nathalie. "No doubt he got an awful lot of points for it, if anyone's keeping track."

"Daemons are in charge of the tempting," said Jason to Laura in a stage-whisper. "It's what we do. The angels try and save people; we try and make them fall."

Laura looked him up and down. She moved a half-step closer to Nathalie.

"But, as you said, your wings are cut now, too…" Jason smiled at them. "So I suppose that makes Nathalie here a daemon, just like me."

"I'm not a daemon," said Nathalie. "I'm a something else."

Jason snorted.

"Fine, I understand. It took me some time to accept things as they were, too, if I remember rightly."

Laura and Blake exchanged glances, but Nathalie shook her head.

"No," she said flatly, "I'm not like you. You chose to be on the wrong side rather than be on no side. I'm not doing that. I'm being on my *own* side. And I'll do better work on my own, here and now, than I ever did in three thousand years of serving the Establishment."

Silence stretched.

"So you two…you knew each other before…before you had your wings cut off?" asked Blake at length.

Jason wheeled to face him, and fixed him with his shark's grin.

"Oh, yes!" he said. "We were great friends! Always working together, always playing together. It seemed to last forever, but actually it couldn't have been longer than, what? Six, seven hundred years?"

"About that, yes," said Nathalie softly.

"We had a lot of good times," Jason went on. "We used to pick a town and spend twenty or thirty years really cleaning it up, making it a really *good* place. Very satisfying work. Or at least, it would have been, if things didn't fall apart so easily…"

"You haven't come here to talk about the past," said Nathalie, who remembered very well how easily things fell apart, who remembered the frustration as well as the satisfaction, and even now could picture the endless emerald feathers raining down, the blood and the shadows and the red blooms in the snow where Jason had fallen.

"You're right," said Jason. "I've come to talk about the future."

He was not smiling any more, and his face looked stern and strange.

"I've come to warn you that what you do is foolish," he said simply. "It won't work, and you'll make enemies of those who might otherwise be your allies. You talk of being on your own side, but you know as well as I do what happens to the friendless when the cold winds blow. The line you are walking is very fine. Finer than you know."

Nathalie opened her mouth, but it was Laura who answered him.

"You're talking about Nathalie teaming up with you?" she said, and her mouth twisted in a disbelieving smile. "You? Excuse me, I realise I don't know you from Adam, but am I not right in thinking that you were the one who got her wings chopped off?"

"I didn't get them chopped off, I told you…" began Jason, but Laura cut him off.

"Yeah, I heard, you *tempted* her," she said. "You think that makes a difference? You were her friend, and you betrayed her. And now you're trying to scare her into joining you. Which basically means, giving up. Giving up on helping people, and trying to screw them instead. If you think she'll do that, you don't know her very well. You might have been her best mate for seven hundred years, but I've only known her for, like, a week, and I know she'd *never* give up," she paused, looked him up and down. "She'd never become like you."

Jason took a deep breath, and fixed Laura with his smile. She suddenly realized that he was paying her complete attention. He had noticed her before, but this was different. This was like there was no one else in the room but the two of them. She couldn't tear her eyes away. Everything else seemed to fade into the distance

"You're quite an expert on giving up, aren't you Laura?" he said it softly, but his words were clear and they carried weight.

"This isn't about me," she said.

"No?" said Jason. "That's not what you told Blake the other night. The other night it wasn't about him, it was all about you.

It was all about how you couldn't take it any more, about how all you wanted was darkness and an end. An end to knowing what your mother had done, or failed to do. Or was it about what *you* had failed to do?"

He tilted his head at her.

"You know, I honestly cannot say which it is," he gave her a sad little smile. "You must be awfully confused yourself, otherwise I would know for sure. So maybe it wasn't about giving up. Maybe it was about punishing yourself."

Laura's face had gone very hard.

"You shut up," she told him. "What I did or didn't do *is over*. I got through it. It's gone."

"Oh, my dear, you didn't get through anything!" Jason laughed softly. "You didn't beat it, you ran away! Tell me, has your mother even noticed you're gone yet?"

Laura tried to speak, but no words would come.

"Of course she hasn't!" Jason went on. "She hasn't been to visit Will since it all happened, and that's because she doesn't miss him. She doesn't miss you, either. She simply doesn't care."

"Leave her alone, Jason," warned Nathalie, stepping closer.

"Or what, my friend?" he asked, his voice still honey and poison. "You're not an angel any more. Best to remember that. I've had a hundred and seventy years to get used to this skin. You think you can beat me as easily as when we last met? Do you really want to try?"

"It's OK," said Laura. "It's just words. It's just what he is. Let him speak, if that's what he wants. His words aren't anything. They're just words."

Her voice was hoarse, though, and Jason was still smiling.

He moved forward half a step, and leant in close.

"Let me give you some advice, my sweet one," he whispered, and she could feel the warmth of his body next to hers. "Whether you're swilling sleeping pills and vodka in the back of a rusty car, or helping some crazy ex-angel organise a sort of supernatural anti-sin club, what it comes down to is this: you're still running."

He leant away from her and straightened his suit.

"And if you get tired of running, well, just give me a shout."

He nodded to Blake, tipped Nathalie a wink, and vanished in a seething puff of black vapor.

Laura let out a sigh.

"I don't want to be rude about your friends, Nathalie," said Blake. "But I think that guy's a bit of a dick."

«««—»»»

The days passed, as days do. Nathalie worked, and Blake and Laura worked for Nathalie. They helped her with little things. They kept the offices clean, they organized the electricity and water bills, they bought the food and cooked the meals.

They did not see Jason again, though that did not mean that he did not see them.

Usually, Nathalie would go to her work alone. Sometimes she asked if one or the other of them would come with.

Blake would usually say no.

Laura would often say yes.

She felt she was changing. She was learning something, though quite what it was, she was too afraid to ask herself. She hardly dared to hope.

«««—»»»

"You have to be aware, there are tendencies, and there are tipping points," said Nathalie, her voice echoing in the darkness.

Laura nodded. She thought she understood. It was damp down here, and the air was stale. At least it wasn't cold, though. There was lots of insulation, and they had had to come through two makeshift airlocks to get here. They couldn't hear much from the world outside. It was all muffled and hushed.

"Everyone thinks things," she went on. "Everyone thinks about doing something bad every now and then. Some people even think about it *a lot*."

61

She shrugged her shoulders, and took a bite out of the apple she was holding.

"That doesn't make them *evil*," she said, crunching loudly and speaking with her mouth open, "So you have to understand, it's not about *thought*. What it's about is actions. And specifically, actions that take place at the tipping point. The first step. The moment the trip becomes the plunge. The moment of no return. That's the point when we act."

Laura peered into the gloomy room, trying to make out the objects kept here. It was a fairly bare space, really. There were two cupboards, and a shelf in one corner. There was a bed.

Then there was the big, thick door with the heavy iron lock.

Something shifted outside. It sounded very distant and far off, but then the insulation was very good. Someone was coming closer.

"Some of the angels—the really old ones—they'd pride themselves on only ever choosing the most exact and perfect moment to show themselves," she said it musingly, waving the apple core about slowly in the air. "That's how skilful they felt they were. They thought they could just show up at this exact right moment, and Pop! Suddenly all those sinful thoughts would vanish!" Nathalie shook her head. "I was never that exact," she went on, shaking her head. "If something needed doing, I would jump straight in. Wasn't afraid to get my hands dirty, as it were. They all saw that as a bit of a problem, the others, the other angels. Not me."

She flashed Laura a smile.

"I believe in direct action."

There was a clicking noise, and the heavy iron door swung open.

The man who stepped in was not quite fat. He was husky, tall, broad, shuffling; he reminded Laura of a big slow bear, with dark thick-rimmed glasses and shaggy hair.

He had a girl slung over one shoulder. Her eyes were closed, and her breathing was shallow.

Laura tensed and surged to her feet. Her heart was hammering very fast in her chest.

"Don't worry, don't do anything hasty," said Nathalie, laying a hand on her shoulder and casually flicking her apple core into the corner of the room.

The man paused in the act of unloading the girl onto the bed, confused by the sound of the apple bouncing to the floor.

"He can't see us, can't hear us either," Nathalie explained. "Or rather, I'm making sure he forgets that we are here before he's even really registered it."

It seemed to be true. The bear-man was acting as if he were all alone apart from the sleeping girl. He laid her gently on the bed. He began to unlace her shoes.

Nathalie got to her feet and looked the man up and down.

"Can you feel it?" she asked Laura, looking her suddenly in the eye.

Laura tilted her head. What was Nathalie talking about?

"Feel what?" she asked.

"The battle going on," she said. "*In here.*" She reached an arm around the broad chest of the man and thumped him on the breast. If he felt it, he gave no sign.

He finished undoing the laces. He slipped one shoe off, then the other. He placed them carefully on the floor.

Laura frowned and shook her head. Of course she couldn't feel…

Nathalie smiled at her.

"Yes," she said, her voice quiet but full of power. "You *can* feel it, can't you?"

Laura strained. It was like trying to listen to the faintest, the most distant and fragile song in the whole world. It was so small and subtle, she was almost sure she was imagining it…

But no.

It was like the sound of a shingle being torn up by the sea. It was like sandpaper rubbing on strong wood, wearing it, wearing it down until little bright beads of blood pricked through…

"I…I'm not sure…" she hesitated. "I can hear…I can feel something…"

Nathalie nodded.

The Fall of the Angel Nathalie

The man finished peeling off the girl's white socks. He tucked them neatly inside her shoes, straightened back up. He stared at her. Her chest rose and fell. A small crescent of flesh showed between the crop of her shirt and the white laces of her sweatpants.

He wants her so much, Laura thought. *He has wanted her so long.*

But he's not evil. He's *not*. He knows this is wrong. He's known it for the last eighteen months, known it every day he's spent down here building this wrong place for wrong thoughts, that has ended up sheltering wrong actions.

And yet he's gone on, day after day, one brick then the next, knowing somewhere in his mind where it was all heading, but not letting himself examine it, not really.

She sighed and closed her eyes, and leant forward. Nathalie cupped her hand and laid it on the man's back, and all at once the feelings and images and knowledge all *sharpened…*

…She could see it she could see it all / all at once and together and piled in tight / one fact on the next as if someone had sliced open his head and every thought had slivered out / moist and loose like raw meat / sliding over her / drowning her in everything he was and wanted and could be…

She saw the house his house where he lived with his (mother) where he grew up now he's old and he's (never had) so alone all he thinks about is (unfair) how he wants but never has can never have (locked outside) never happy never with someone always alone and the girl next door is (her legs / so soft) kind to him / sometimes / treats him like (slender curve soft) a real human touches his arm (her skin on his warm / her lips red) and he wants her so much but she would never (not for him) never touch him let him touch her never lonely wouldn't hurt her doesn't want to hurt her this is (so wrong) what he wants (not / what he wants) digging and laying bricks and insulation (couldn't hear the screams) quiet down here peaceful (all alone / so alone / not alone) I don't want to do this I can't stop this I must not (too late now/ lift up her shirt/ undo the strings) want to (don't) want to

64

(brown soft leg flesh and gentle rising breath) reach out and touch…

Laura shuddered and pulled back.

She shook her head, tried to clear it of the thoughts which did not belong to her.

Nathalie was smiling in the half light.

"You see?" she said. "You can hear these things if you listen. You should be proud. Not everyone can do what you just did, hear what you just heard."

Laura felt like she might be sick.

Behind Nathalie, the bear-man leant down towards the girl. One of his damp hands reached out towards the white lace bow that was strung tight around her sweatpants.

Nathalie took a deep breath.

"Like I mentioned," she said. "There are tendencies…and there are tipping points."

She grasped Laura's hand, softly, but there was a strength behind the silk that could not be resisted.

"Lesson one is to listen," Nathalie told her as she gently forced her hand towards the bear-man's back. "Lesson two is to speak. But when you speak, you use their voice and their words, and that way they must understand…"

Laura's hand connected with his back, and suddenly the whirl of his thoughts caught her up again…

…only now she could feel Nathalie in there, too, not just watching the pillars and dripping columns of thought and memory and desire as they arched and heaved around them, but directing them, too, pushing and tugging and *forming* them up out of the phosphorescent stuff of raw mind that comprised his internal world, and it was like—

—the sweet warmth of the girl's skin as my hand brushes the flesh and my need pulses up, roaring, drowning everything else, smothering the faint echo of (wrong this is wrong / don't / pull back) but then just before that is lost forever a hand that is not mine reaches deep within me and heaves it back and the (wrong wrong — stop stop) is swirling back past me, shooting up next to the desire and now the cages are — swapped — and now the (I want her I want those browned skin red lips moist fullness of her I want) what am I doing how can I be doing this — not me this is not me I was not made to do this (she sleeps how easy it would be to) I am not going to do this because I see it all at once, all the things that would (touch undress caress) come to pass if I followed this to the bitter end

three moments of animal pleasure

heavy breathing after in the dark

sleeping her body sleeping oblivious

no way out but one

metal glinting in the raw orange light

her waking to the darkness and the stillness and my blood

her fingers bleeding raw trying to leave this place

escape the cool night the homecoming the sirens

ruined everything ruined everything

broken

—and I breathe in suddenly like coming out of deep water and I feel free because I know what I must do and because that small poison is now (GONE) burnt clean and rubbed clear and the space where it was is so empty I don't even know what it was because it is (GONE) and I cannot see that part of me any more I am glad I am so happy because that (GONE) part of me has been taken away and now I am free—

Laura staggered backwards, and it was only Nathalie gripping her hand that kept her from falling.

Externally, nothing seemed to have changed. The bear-man still hunched over the sleeping figure of the girl on the bed. But she knew. She had seen it, she had *lived it*.

They had been there, right inside his mind.

They had changed it. They had altered him.

"Yes, we have," said Nathalie, and her teeth shone white in the darkness. "I have now such a tiny fraction of the power I held when I was an angel, and yet...I have never acted so cleanly, never been able to do my job as well as I can now..."

She spoke almost as if talking to herself.

"What did you...what was that?" Laura asked.

"You saw as well as I did," said Nathalie. "In fact, you helped. We took what was wrong in him, what was dangerous, what was damaging. We took it all and we wrapped it up tight and locked it in iron and bound it firm and then...then we burnt it away to nothing."

Her voice was confident, but was there something there...

She didn't know she was going to do that, Laura thought suddenly.

She meant to take away his thoughts, take away his desire... but she hadn't meant to destroy *them. She meant to bury them, not burn them.*

The moment she thought it, she knew it was true.

Her eyes darted to Nathalie, but Nathalie was far away, and if she had heard what Laura had thought, she gave no sign.

Laura turned her thoughts inwards, and she saw it. She saw her own mind as clearly as she had seen the bear-man's. It was so obvious. How could she have not been aware of it before?

The source of her own thoughts, the secret fire that burnt within her, burnt in the middle of her mind, and cast its flickering shadows outwards into the world for anyone who had the talent to read them...

The shadows of her thoughts were dancing over Nathalie; it was only because Nathalie was lost in her own that she had not spotted them...

Laura silenced her mind, pushing her wonderings and doubts to one side.

Why had she done that? She did not know. She just felt instinctively that she did not want Nathalie to see how much she had understood...

The hunched form of the bear-man straightened up.

His breathing was steady, but there were tears in his eyes.

"Come on," said Nathalie. "It's time for us to go."

She led them through the heavy door and into the clean air outside.

As they left, the bear-man began to dress the girl in the darkness, while his thoughts lurched awkwardly around the gaping wound in his mind, and the tears rolled down his cheeks.

«‹‹—››»

"Maybe she's rubbing off on you," said Blake. He lifted his hand to touch her shoulder, hesitated, let it fall back to his side.

A jogger ran past, his dog following excitedly at his heels, and Laura stepped to one side to let them by.

The sun shone brightly on the park, warming March to spring, and making Blake sweat inside his padded jacket.

Laura harrumphed to herself and made a face.

"Maybe," she said at length. She had told him about the man in the bunker, about how Nathalie had somehow taken them both inside his thoughts...and then how she had burnt out those thoughts she had deemed harmful.

But none of that worried Blake as much as the last point.

How later, after they had come back into the light, and for a short time only, Laura had been able to look into other people, too. People she passed in the street, people who she walked near to, people who served her at the supermarket when she was buying food. She couldn't read them as clearly as she had the bear-man, down beneath the earth, with no one else to confuse things, and Nathalie there to help her. But that wasn't the point.

She had been able to understand what people were thinking. She could see into them.

It troubled him.

"I think you should stop going with her," he said at length, and rushed on before she could interrupt him. "It's obviously having *some* effect on you, Laura," he said. "Who knows where it'll end?"

"I told you, it's gone away now, anyway!" She sounded irritated.

"I know," he said. "But what about next time? What if every time you go with her, you get a little bit closer to being…well, being what she is."

"And would that be such a bad thing?" she asked him. "To be an angel?"

"She's not an angel," he told her. "Remember? She's a something else."

She rolled her eyes. A little way ahead of them on the path, a man was throwing something to the ducks. They could hear the sound of splashing as the food hit the water.

"Oh, so you think she's what? A daemon or something?" She shook her head. "Is that what you imagine daemons do? Save girls from being raped, stop wrongs from being committed, stop people from doing evil things? Doesn't sound very daemonic to me."

"That's not it," said Blake. "You said yourself, she was surprised at what she did down there. How far she went." He shrugged. "Maybe she's…losing control."

He got the last words out in a rush before he could stop himself.

"Losing control?" Laura sounded cynical, but her voice shook slightly, and she paused.

"Look," she went on, "she's doing what she set out to, right? She's doing exactly what she told us she would. We've trusted her this far. I mean, if it wasn't for her, I'd be…"

She cut off, as if she hadn't realized where her train of thought had been heading.

69

Blake nodded unhappily. Everything Laura was saying was true, it was just…

They meandered slowly along. They had nearly reached the man feeding the ducks. He was reaching into a paper bag, and throwing little morsels into the river.

"It's just…if she's actually *burning* parts of someone away to stop them doing something," said Blake. "Well, does that mean that they wouldn't have done it? I mean, just because they didn't do it, it wasn't because they *chose* not to. It was because…why have you stopped?"

But Laura wasn't listening to him. She had pulled up short. She was staring at the man ahead of them on the path.

Blake followed her gaze. Something was dripping from the damp bottom of the paper bag. It was falling to the grass, staining the green blades crimson.

As they watched, the man reached another hand into the bag, pulled out a lump of raw, dripping meat, and threw it into the lake. One of the ducks flapped up above the others, opened its beak, and caught the chunk of gristle in one fluid *snap*. In the water, a few tendrils of swirling blood spoke of other lumps of meat that had not been snapped up so quickly.

Blake looked back to the man. He noticed suddenly how well-dressed he was. The sunglasses were not incongruous in the bright sunlight, but the suit was very sharp.

"I know exactly what you mean, Blake," said Jason, fishing the last lump of meat out and throwing it amid the ducks, before licking the empty bag carefully, folding it, and placing it back in a pocket. "If someone has no *choice*, well, where's the fun in that?"

He grinned at them.

"Though I must say, it has been rather interesting to watch her working style, uh, evolve." He turned to face them full on. He peered at them over his sunglasses, and Blake got the faint impression of poisonous yellow eyes staring out at him. "You can't believe how boring it was to watch her work before. Trust me. I worked with her for seven hundred years. I speak from experience: she was *dull*."

"What do you want?" Laura said the words flatly, but Blake could feel her bristling.

Jason spread his hands.

"Just to talk," he said innocently. "I just wondered how things were going, that's all."

"Well, you've heard more than you were meant to," said Laura. "You were lucky. Why don't you bugger off while the going's good?"

Jason laughed, loudly, and clapped his hands as if she'd just said the funniest thing in the world.

"Oh, I *like* this one!" he said to Blake. "You actually said that like a threat! My, what fun! I haven't come across a human as spirited as you for quite some time, I must say."

He wiped an imaginary tear from the corner of his eye with an exquisitely white handkerchief.

"Now," he said, suddenly serious, steepling his hands and resting them under his chin. "Have you thought any more about what we said, Laura? Have you grown tired of running, yet? Ready to confront things? I say this purely so that you know I am here to help."

"She doesn't want anything to do with you," Blake told him. He tried to make his voice deep, but it sounded reedy in his own ears.

"Not talking to you, mouse boy," snapped Jason, pointing a manicured finger at him. "And if you don't stay quiet when your betters are speaking, I'll take your voice away forever."

He leant in close, and levered his smile up a notch.

"I'm not talking figuratively, either," he whispered, pulling his sunglasses down for a moment, so that Blake could see the bright yellow of his eyes. "I'll literally take your voice away. You'll never speak again. It's one of the things I can do. So just stay quiet for a minute, huh?"

"Don't you *threaten* him!" said Laura. "Don't you threaten *any* of us!"

Jason smiled, and darted his eyes to her. He opened his mouth as if to speak, frowned, and closed it again.

"Hmm," he said at length, one eyebrow flicking up. "Looks like Nathalie's not the only one who's been…stretching herself. And yet…"

Laura suddenly shuddered, clasped one hand to her head.

"You put up these little walls, not realising how thin the paper is," Jason chuckled to himself.

"It's impressive, though, really it is," he went on. "It's not one human in ten thousand who can properly shield their thoughts from me. That you were trying at all is remarkable. Pointless, but remarkable. So Nathalie has found herself a little acolyte, has she? How interesting."

"I'm not her acolyte," said Laura. "I'm her friend."

"Our kind don't have room for friends," said Jason, reproachfully. "Clients—yes; colleagues—yes. But friends? Our kind does not keep them."

"Not your kind, maybe. Hers does."

Jason shrugged.

"We're the same," he said simply. "The sooner she realises that, the more painless it will be for everyone. Yourselves included."

He turned as if to leave, hesitated, and spoke over his shoulder.

"Oh, by the way," he said, "the answer to what you were wondering, Blake: yes, Nathalie is rubbing off on your little friend here. Or rather, she's opening her up to what she has the potential to be. Dangerous game though, opening someone up. You never know what might come spilling out."

"Just go away," said Blake. "Just get gone."

Jason leant his head to one side.

"You know," he pondered, "maybe I won't take your voice away. Maybe I'll just take all of you away. Break you into lots of little bits, and leave you somewhere far away and lonely. Somewhere that you can die slowly, and your screams won't disturb anyone but the birds."

Blake swallowed.

He opened his mouth to say something, but Jason was gone.

A few strands of vapor hung in the air for a moment before floating away on the breeze.

"A flower, opening," said Nathalie, and inhaled deeply on her cigarette. "Your turn."

Laura nodded. She screwed up her eyes, but nothing came to mind.

"Remember, don't force it," said Nathalie. "You're not trying to ram your way in. Not this time, not when I'm letting you inside. Just relax. Just try to see it. And here, hold my hand."

"I thought you said you don't have to be touching," said Laura.

"We don't," said Nathalie. "But it will help you focus. So now: what am I thinking."

Laura tried to relax. They had been practising for the last two hours, but it was discouraging work. Sometimes, something seemed to *click* in her mind, and for a moment or two it worked, and she could almost see what it was Nathalie was thinking. But more often than not what came to her mind was either completely wrong or—more often—a depressing, empty blankness.

"Uh…a pair of pliers," she hazarded.

"No. Again."

"The street performers in Covent Garden, on a hot day in June."

"That's what you're thinking of, not me. Again."

"How you always wanted to learn more about computers, and now at last you might have time."

"Wrong!" said Nathalie. "Stop guessing! And for your information, I already know quite a lot about computers, thank you."

Laura threw up her arms in frustration, and struggled to her feet.

"This is stupid, anyway!" she said, pacing up and down the small front room of their office in Dulwich. "How will being able to read him stop him from seeing into me? I need to know how to shield myself, not see into him!"

"I told you, we're coming to that," said Nathalie. "They're linked, don't you see? Could you learn to write without learning to read? First, you get used to looking into other people. Then, knowing what it means to do that, you imagine what other people see when they look into you. Finally, you learn how to block it. Now sit down."

"How do we know Jason's even interested in me anyway?" she said, still standing, arms crossed tightly. "You said yourself that he's probably just using me to get to you."

"I don't need to be able to read your mind to know you don't believe that," said Nathalie flatly. "Sit."

Laura shook her head; but she crossed her legs again, and lowered herself down next to Nathalie.

"Have you been practising with Blake like I told you?" asked Nathalie.

"Well, a bit. Sort of," admitted Laura.

"What do you mean? Either you have or you haven't."

"I got it right," she said brightly, then sighed. "That was the problem. I kept getting it right. Wasn't much variation in what he was thinking. I don't think he was trying to. But it got embarrassing after a while."

"There you go then!" enthused Nathalie.

Laura shook her head.

"No. Not much difference from normal, really. I mean, I often used to have a pretty good idea when he was…thinking about me."

Nathalie raised an eyebrow.

"You're right. Maybe you should just practice with me."

Laura sighed.

"A…feather," she tried.

Nathalie smiled.

"Close," she said.

««—»»

Several miles away, in a small, brightly lit room filled with needles and bandages and bags of sterile fluid, the air began to seethe. Black mist wrapped itself out of nothing, flared, coalesced into a tall, humanoid figure.

No one was there to see this happen; however, if they had been, they surely would have noticed the exquisite cut of the suit the figure wore, as well as passing comment on the unsettling smell that came with him. It was a smell that seemed familiar, though you wouldn't have been able to have said quite why. It was what hope smells like, the moment the bubble bursts and the stuff inside starts to sour. It was what the first day of spring smells like, when winter flashes back through the chill morning air and slays all the budding flowers.

The figure examined himself critically in the mirror, made a few minor adjustments to the line of his jaw and the shade of his skin, and walked out onto the ward.

Everyone recognized the great surgeon as he stalked past. A few even dared to greet him, and quickly reeled back from the poisonous glares they received in return.

When he located the bed he wanted, the man who everyone thought was the great surgeon pulled the curtains round. No one stopped him, of course.

He examined the figure on the bed critically.

"Yes," he conceded at length. "I suppose I can see the resemblance."

«««—»»»

Laura watched her mother walk across the water towards her, and felt a red mist of anger rise, even though she knew it wasn't real. Seeing Suzanne always made her feel furious. It had done for almost as long as she could remember, even before she stopped thinking of her as mother.

No, she thought, *that's not what's there.*

She closed her eyes so tightly colors flashed in front of her; but when she opened them, her mother was still there.

"That's not the way," Suzanne told her. "Remember? Like we said. The problem's not out here, not out in the world. It's what I'm doing to your mind…Try and find it…"

Laura took a breath, held it, let the air hiss out between her teeth.

The Fall of the Angel Nathalie

She let her awareness of the world around her contract inwards, like a bubble with all the air being sucked out, until it extended just a little way from her, then wrapped her body, then finally just encircled her mind. A wave of peace washed through her. She felt so light she wondered if she might float away.

Just me, she thought.

Just me in the stillness.

And then she realized that wasn't true.

She could feel the tendril of *other* reaching into her mind.

It was so thin, so subtle and strange she could hardly even be sure it was there.

It's there, though, she thought.

It's her.

She pushed against the alien tendril of thought. She felt it hovering in her mind, followed it inwards to where it pushed and pulsed against things within her, caressing and awakening memories and images she hadn't even known she possessed.

Manipulating them.

She found a casket that had been eased open. It contained an image of her mother.

Her eyes shot open.

It was the same image of her mother that now walked across the water towards her.

She eased against the tendril questing into her mind, and the image flickered.

Her mother smiled—

—and became Nathalie for a moment—

—then flashed back to being her mother.

"Good," said Suzanne, but the voice was wrong. It was distorted, heavy, as if something was breaking. "You've found where I got in. You've seen what I've tapped into. Now…undo it."

Laura licked her lips.

This was always the part she struggled with.

She could usually find the presence in her mind—almost always in fact, even if it took her a few moments to do so—and Nathalie had been growing increasingly subtle, using thinner and

76

thinner strands of influence, sometimes even wrapping them in kaleidoscopic patterns around hidden bends and switchbacks in her mind that Laura did not even know she had, making it more and more difficult to identify and trace.

But she was still able to find them, however much care Nathalie chose to use.

Undoing the weave, however…Ah, now that was trickier…

She moved her awareness inwards again. She found the point where the radiating projections of the presence in her mind were burrowing their way into her memories…

…She took a deep breath…

…And she slammed the lid shut on the casket where those thoughts were held.

The mother-skin Nathalie had projected over her body within Laura's perceptions shuddered, flickered, faded…died.

Laura choked back a laugh. She had done it!

"Excellent!" said Nathalie. "And the waves…?"

"Wait…" said Laura.

The second wave was easier to find, and once found, easier to sever.

The waves pulsed upwards in a crash of grey-blue spray, faltered, dissolved down to the gently swaying green of the grass on which Nathalie was truly walking.

Nathalie skipped the last few steps to her side, and embraced her.

"Well done!" she said. "That's quicker than you've ever managed before! Two separate illusions, and I made both of them difficult. You should be proud! Do you feel proud?"

Laura just felt relieved.

Ever since Jason had surprised them in the park, over a month ago, she had felt vulnerable, horribly, achingly vulnerable.

If he could appear there in the park…then where was safe?

Nowhere. Not while her own mind went unguarded, at any rate…

"I can't believe I actually did it," said Laura. "You were really trying, weren't you? You weren't just holding back, trying to give me confidence?"

Nathalie shook her head.

"That was me working pretty hard, I can assure you," she said. "You have to remember what I keep telling you, Laura: you're a natural at this. I've scarcely met anyone with more potential. And I've been around a fair while, I can tell you. I've seen things. I've seen people."

Laura's smile faltered. She knew what was coming next, and she never cared to hear it.

It scared her.

I don't want to be chosen, she thought.

Nathalie put an arm on her shoulder. Her face softened.

"I know," she said softly. "And I'm not choosing you. Neither is anyone else. You're mine anyway; the Establishment can't have you!"

Laura smiled, but something inside her felt cold.

Deep down, she wasn't quite sure how much she wanted to belong to Nathalie, either.

«««——»»»

"So what, are you an angel now, too?" asked Blake.

He inspected a bunch of bananas critically, tore off the most withered looking, and deposited the reminder into their shopping trolley.

"Don't be an idiot," replied Laura. "She's not an angel, is she? How could I be one?"

"OK, so you're a something else as well, then?"

Laura rolled her eyes.

"No, I'm not an angel or a something else," she said, as patiently as she could manage. "I'm a Laura, that's it. Nothing's changed."

Blake shook his head, tried to bury his annoyance.

Of course something had changed!

"It hasn't," said Laura.

"It bloody well has!" said Blake, angrily heaving a crate of cat food into the trolley. "I mean, you could at least wait for me to say something before you answer it!"

"Why have you done that? We haven't even got a cat!"

Blake seethed silently for a moment, snorted, and replaced the cat food on the shelf.

"All I'm saying is, it makes me a bit uncomfortable, that's all!"

"I'm not poking around in there, you know!" protested Laura. "I'm hardly doing anything. It's just the little bits skimming about on the surface, the things I can't help but see."

There was a buzzing noise from Laura's pocket. She pulled out her mobile phone and grimaced.

"The hospital," she said. "No, not today."

She pressed the cancel button and shoved the phone away.

Blake took a deep breath, shook his head, gave her a half-smile.

"OK, I guess I just don't like feeling left out."

Laura nodded.

"I can understand that," she said.

"I just wish I could be more involved in this new…this new thing you've got going on."

They rounded a corner, and made for the checkouts.

"So what, can you hear what everyone in this queue is thinking, then?" asked Blake, quite loudly.

Laura frowned at him.

"Not here," she hissed.

"Oh, I see," said Blake. "So you're allowed to look into anyone's mind you feel like, and I'm not even supposed to talk about it? Very fair."

He turned his back on her, and started talking to the woman in front of him.

"Excuse me," he said. "I'm sorry to bother you, it's just I wanted to let you know that the lady behind me can read thoughts. So, you know, if you were thinking about anything secret or…or guilty or whatever, just, you know…" He made a little softening motion with his hands.

"Maybe you can ask her to tell you what I'm thinking about you, then," said the woman.

"What a charming lady," muttered Blake, then turned back to Laura.

"Anyway," he went on, "how does it even work? I mean, I'm thinking lots of things, all at once. Some things, I don't even *realise* I'm thinking them, because the other thoughts are so much bigger and get in the way. I get confused enough just dealing with my own thoughts. Having to think for two is actually quite a worrying thought, when you think about it."

Laura's phone started buzzing again. She pulled it out, frowned at the screen for a moment, and put it away unanswered.

"Why the hell do they keep calling *me*?" she said. "*She's* the one they need to be talking to."

The woman in front of them finished paying, and the man at the till started scanning their shopping through.

"What do *you* think about mind reading?" Blake asked him, as he started bagging up their items.

The man shrugged.

"You tell me," he said.

"Smartarse," Blake muttered.

They finished packing in silence.

"I've just gotta go to the toilet," said Blake. "I mean, I'm sure you know that. But I thought I'd let you know. For the look of things."

Laura rolled her eyes.

"Fine," she said. "I suppose I should call them back anyway."

She pulled out her phone, and Blake left her to find the toilet.

When he returned a few moments later, the trolley containing their shopping stood forlornly next to the checkout.

Laura was nowhere to be seen.

««——»»

The words washed over her, but none of them seemed to stick.

One of the doctors offered her a box of tissues, but it wasn't sadness she felt, and her eyes were dry as sand.

80

"He was comfortable at the end," they said.

"At least he didn't suffer," they said.

"What quality of life did he have?" they asked her.

Laura felt something shifting and growing inside of her. It had been there so long, she had almost forgotten it was there, almost forgotten the world could be any different. But it had been still for so long…How had she forgotten it was there?

Her hands did not shake, and her eyes were very dry.

"He took a turn for the worse two nights ago," they explained.

"Sometimes in these situations, a palliative approach is best."

The doctors nodded at one another. They wanted her to nod, too.

The pain rose in waves. It felt so sharp and fresh. It was like waking up.

Where had she been?

How could she have forgotten this?

"As you know, up until now, we had felt—as a team—that it was worth continuing with active treatment," they told her. "But when William developed this latest infection, we just felt that enough was enough. Given his situation, why put him through more?"

Everything else, her time with Nathalie…it had all been wrong.

Jason had known the truth.

It had all been running away.

"We contacted your mother," the older doctor said. "She was next of kin. It wasn't her decision, of course, but we were glad that she agreed with our approach."

Something tightened in Laura. The weight she had carried for so long teetered, the balance shifting. Laura closed her eyes.

"We tried to contact her again regarding the paperwork," the doctor went on. "But she said she was too busy. She suggested we get in touch with you. Which is what we did, of course."

Laura stayed very still.

She opened her eyes.

"Don't worry," she said. "I'll explain to her how important this all is."

THE FALL OF THE ANGEL NATHALIE

They were surprised when she got up so suddenly, but no one tried to stop her.

It was only natural, they told one another.

After all, anger was part of the grieving process.

«««——»»»

He couldn't believe she had left without him.

He couldn't believe she had just run off.

Blake stalked home through the gusts of wind and the first cold drops of the coming downpour.

It was so typical of how things had become.

She was always with Nathalie. She was always running off, chasing her own adventures, learning these strange new things about herself.

She always left him.

He did the shopping, paid the bills, cooked the meals.

She had stopped telling him where she went or why.

The bags were so heavy. She had all the money on her. He didn't have enough on him to order a taxi.

Across the road, unnoticed by Blake amid the pouring rain and the roiling of his own dark thoughts, a figure in a fine tailored suit adjusted his sunglasses and watched the young man walk away. He smiled to himself.

Well then, let her go, Blake thought as he set his shoulders and quickened his pace, *I'm damned if I'm going chasing after her again.*

«««——»»»

There was a city, and in that city was a street. In the street there was a house, and approaching the door of the house was a small body, very thin and miserable.

And angry.

The rain was falling hard, but Laura barely felt it.

She knew what she had to do. She thought she had known it all along.

The house loomed large before her. Downstairs, all was dark, but light shone from a window above, and Laura knew it was not empty.

Her hand tightened in her pocket.

I didn't throw the key away, she thought.

I knew I would need it. I knew that one day I would come back.

She hesitated a few steps from the front door.

Once she had opened it, she knew, there was no turning back.

There was already no turning back.

There never was.

She took a step forward, and the air seethed black in front of her.

The darkness shifted.

A figure stepped out of the night.

It was Nathalie.

She looked taller, somehow. Her face was set and grim.

"What are you doing here, Laura?" she asked quietly.

Her eyes were burning yellow, but Laura met them and did not flinch.

"I've come to finish things," she said.

Nathalie spread her hands.

"They're finished already," she said. "Remember? That person you were, the one who carried all that hate, all that anger…she died when I fell to earth. You came with me, and you were reborn. Just like I was. You don't have to be that person. You are clean."

Laura laughed then, but it sounded hollow.

"He was right, Nathalie. Jason was right. All I've been doing is running. I hate her for what she did, for what she let happen. But I've never faced her. All I've done is run away, and pretend it never happened. And that's not enough."

Nathalie was standing very still. The wind clutched the rain, hurled it at them.

"You're not going in there," Nathalie told her flatly. "If you hurt her, you maim yourself. I won't let you do that."

Laura's cheek tugged into a half-smile.

"You want to save me now, too, is that it?" she asked.

"No," said Nathalie, shaking her head. "I've already saved you. I'm not letting you undo that."

"And don't I get a choice about that?"

"It's not about choice," said Nathalie. "You think *you've* chosen this? Jason is very good at leading people. At *tempting* people. It's what he does. It's what he did to me."

But Laura was shaking her head.

"No one's forcing my hand," she said. "Not Jason, not you. Blake talked me out of confronting her once before, but I was wrong to let him. It's not his decision. It's no one's decision but mine. Now get out of my way. I'm going to talk to my mother."

Lightning flashed above them, and a moment later thunder shook the air. In the sudden, blinding darkness that followed, Nathalie's eyes glowed yellow venom in the black threshold of the house.

"I'm sorry it has to be this way," said Nathalie.

She tilted her head to one side—

—and suddenly she was there, inside Laura's mind. She could feel the cloying tendrils of her thought, flashing inside her brain, faster and subtler than she had ever believed possible, darting in a thousand directions at once. She felt the core of her splayed open, every thought and memory laid bare—

Laura reeled backwards, stumbled to one knee. Her hands shot up to cradle her head. She felt that it might explode. She opened her mouth to scream and nothing came out and—

—the caskets of her mind were being sprung open, one and then the next, quicker than she could comprehend, *snap, snap, snap*, opened and inspected and discarded, until finally—

She could not breathe. The world swum around her. In the background, she had the faintest impression of a man strolling across the street towards them. She could see Nathalie's yellow eyes reflected in the polished darkness of his sunglasses. She scrabbled at the ground, tried to make the world stand still, and then—

—the locked vault inside her creaked and opened, and there it was inside, all bound together with hate and fear and venom: the memories Nathalie was looking for, the things that had happened to Will, and that she had done and had not done, the poison and the engine of her soul. Nathalie flowed around it. She lifted it, held it up in the brightness of her thought, inspected it cool and close and careful. And then something *sparked*. A new tendril of thought was arching out from Nathalie, coiled and white-hot and deadly. It swam towards the part of Laura's mind that Nathalie was holding up, pulling open, extended and vulnerable like a throat ripe for slitting. It came closer, closer, and Laura could feel the awful heat of it, and—

The man in the sunglasses stopped walking towards them. He smiled at Laura, over Nathalie's shoulder, and…

This is not the way, she suddenly knew.

Laura stopped fighting.

Her dark eyes met the yellow ones locked on her face, and she felt everything tighten to a single point of concentration located in the utter stillness of her mind—

—and she forced Nathalie's poison back. She clasped the deadly heat of it, held it tight an inch and a mile and the thickness of a thought from the tender pulsing mass of her memories, of her substance and her core, of the things in her that were *hers alone*.

No, she thought.

The world creaked and strained.

Everything trembled, toppled…

…and with a silent explosion, all the casks in her mind slammed shut, and a key turned very tight. A wave of chaos shot back through all the tendrils that had ransacked her mind and—

Nathalie stumbled backwards. She fell into the door and slid sideways, half collapsing into the street.

Her eyes widened.

"*How dare you?*" Laura hissed at her. "If you take these things from us, then what's left? Happy little puppets of flesh with wide smiles and broken minds?"

Laura drew the key out of her pocket and stepped up to the door.

She turned the key in the lock.

"Goodbye, Nathalie," she said, and stepped into the darkness. She closed the door behind her.

Nathalie slumped in the road.

The rain fell fast around her, and the ground was very cold.

She staggered to her feet, and reached out for the door.

A hand clasped her gently by the shoulder.

"Now, now," said a voice she recognized. "Let's let the humans play amongst themselves for a while."

《《—》》

It was dark inside the house, but Laura knew it well. She had grown up here. She knew every inch, every step and corner.

The sound of a television, muffled by walls and doors and distance, swam down to her from a room above. She moved softly through the sleeping house.

She thought of the last time she had been in this house. It was when she had darted in to grab the blanket with which she had covered Nathalie after she had fallen, naked and bleeding, out of the sky and into her life.

She had hardly thought of the place since then. She had not dared.

Up the stairs she went. They were old, and creaked beneath her feet, but if anyone heard, no one took any notice.

Have they even realized I've been gone? She wondered.

At the top of the stairs she paused. The television was louder here. She could see the flickering light of it, dancing under the door at the end of the hall.

That was the door she wanted.

That was the door to her mother's room.

She thought of all the times she had walked this hallway before. Creeping along it on awkward legs as a toddler, awkward, clinging onto her father's trousers to balance. Then her father had left, and she'd had to learn to stand on her own. That was the clearest thing she could remember about him: the fold of his trousers that had been at eye level, the fold she clung onto with her soft little fingers.

When Max had come, she had been able to walk quite well enough without someone to help her. Not that Max would have offered to help. He had never been nasty to her; he had never really cared enough to hate her.

She had dashed along the hallway, too, as a teenager late for school, hurrying to the bathroom to get ready.

And she played here with Will. They had played all sorts of games, ever since she was old enough to realise that her elder brother was a little…simple. That he never had friends of his own to play with, that their mother hardly cared about him, that she was all he had.

It was a lot of responsibility. It was a lot of weight to carry.

Sometimes, she remembered, it used to make her so angry.

She reached the door, and stopped.

The sound of the television was loud now, blaring and invasive—her mother always liked to have the volume turned up full—and she could not hear anything else from behind the door.

But she knew they were there.

They would all be there, her mother and Max, with King curled up at the foot of the bed.

That's how it always used to be: Suzanne and Max locked away in the bedroom, and Laura having to stay in to look after Will, while her friends went out and got drunk and went on holiday and met boys and went to parties…

Now Will was gone; but her mother was still behind the door, wrapped up in bed with Max; and she was still locked outside and forgotten.

She took a deep breath.

She opened the door and went in.

《《—》》

87

THE FALL OF THE ANGEL NATHALIE

"Let go of me," said Nathalie, trying to shrug Jason's hand away.

But Jason gave a jerk, and suddenly she was staggering back into the rain, and Jason was between her and the door.

"My dear Nathalie," he said, smiling. "I think the girl has made it pretty clear that she doesn't want to be disturbed. Why not stay and talk with me a while?"

"I've got nothing to say to you!" she hissed at him. "Now let me through, before it's too late!"

Jason shook his head sadly.

"Oh, Nathalie," he said. "It's always been too late. Too late for her, too late for you. Best to accept that now."

Nathalie crouched low.

"Get out of my way, or I'll tear you apart," she told him. Her voice was as soft as the pattering of the rain.

Jason spread his hands.

"You're quite welcome to try," he said.

Nathalie showed him her teeth.

Then she launched herself forward.

She moved faster than a human eye could follow; but Jason was no human, and Nathalie was used to being something more than she now was.

He caught her by the wrists, twisted with the movement of her body, and suddenly she was sailing out across the road. Her legs hit the top of a car, and she flipped end over and slammed upside-down into the wall of a house. It crumpled around her, and she fell to the floor in a pile of rubble and dust.

She staggered up again.

"I warned you, Nathalie," Jason called out to her, a singsong lilt in his voice. "You're not an angel anymore. And I have a lot more practice at this than you do."

She snarled, slipped her hands under the car she had clipped with her feet, and flipped it towards him. Jason brought his hands round in a lightning-fast arc, and the car was suddenly tearing in two around him. The two segments crashed down to either side. Jason pulled a pocket watch out of his jacket, inspected it dispassionately, and put it back.

Along the street, lights began to go on in windows, and faces peered out into the night.

"You can rage all you want," Jason told her. "You can huff and puff and blow out your little cheeks. But you're not getting inside that house. Not until your friend there has done what she has wanted so badly to do since the first moment I met her."

Nathalie did not even bother to reply.

She ran again; this time she did not aim for the door.

Jason laughed loud, and leapt to meet her.

«‹‹—››»

The only face that turned to look at her when she opened the door was King's.

He looked up at her quizzically, his big dark eyes reflecting the light of the television, his wet tongue lolling out as he panted.

Max was asleep, his head resting on the pillow, a newspaper folded unread on his lap.

And then there was her mother.

She looked the same as ever. Her peroxide hair was pulled back by a bright pink clip, and her face looked sallow and sick in the washed out light. A smudge of chocolate was melted to her cheek, and her eyes were fixed on the screen.

Laura closed the door behind her.

She picked up the remote control from where it lay by Max, and pressed the mute button.

The silence was so sudden it was as loud as an explosion.

"Hello, mum," said Laura.

«‹‹—››»

Blake tapped his fingers on the kitchen table.

Where were they?

He was getting used to being ignored, but this seemed...different, somehow.

He sighed and turned the television on.

Well, if they wanted to go and play their games and leave him out of it, that was fine with him.

He opened a can of beer and sunk into the sofa.

«««—»»»

"Laura?" Suzanne squinted up at her. "What are you doing here?"

Max stirred in the bed, but did not wake.

Laura smiled.

"I've come to show you what happened to Will," she told her mother.

Suzanne scowled.

Laura centred herself, and reached out.

Her mother's face slackened as Laura drifted inside.

«««—»»»

Nathalie had aimed her jump to reach the upstairs window, but Jason slammed into her in mid-air. They arced up over the houses and landed with a crash on a roof.

"Let me go!" screamed Nathalie, but Jason just laughed.

A mass of loosened tiles slid with them, and they tipped over the lip of the roof and tumbled down into the street below. Nathalie fell on top. She scrambled up and darted away.

Jason sprang after her.

She shot towards the house as fast she could. She had nearly reached it. Her hand was grasping out for the handle...

Jason ploughed into her, and all at once tendrils of darkness were wrapping round her body, sliding into her, forcing her to dissipate, forcing them both to slide out of *here* and slither back to *there*...

«««—»»»

"I want to show you something," said Laura, but the words were redundant.

JAMIE BRINDLE

Her mother's mind opened around her. It stretched away in a vast, ugly landscape, windswept and piled high with rusted things and broken things and buried, half-forgotten useless pained and soiled things.

Laura gaped at how someone could live here.

Tendrils of her awareness shot out to every corner, faster than she had realized she knew how. She was working on instinct, now. It all felt so easy. It all felt so *right*.

She secured the borders, she locked things down. She felt the burning centre of her mother's awareness, and held it tight in her hands.

"What are y—

—*ou doing?* Her mother asked, voice and thoughts merging into something that Laura felt as much as heard.

I am showing you who you are, she told her, twisting the thoughts as they left her mind, making them resonate within her mother. Laura knew that Suzanne could no longer tell where her own thoughts ended and her daughter's began.

She raised a great bar of white-hot thought, a pillar of blankness in the landscape of her mother's mind, and with a heave she swept a space clear. She felt her mother shudder.

I will show you your son, she told her, and reached backwards inside herself with another flicker of thought, and pulled out her memories of Will.

The image shuddered, flexed and flickered as it moved from her mind to Suzanne's, and for a moment everything teetered, and Laura worried that it would burst. But then the landscape stabilized, and they were looking at an image of Will. A perfect image.

It showed him so clearly. It was everything he was and everything he had been. It was everything he could have become.

It was his smiling face and his clumsy hands, it was the corner of his eyes where the tears formed and fell.

This was your son, Laura whispered, soft in the raging silence, so loud and clear and perfect that her mother could not escape the words, nor the accusation that seeped in under them.

THE FALL OF THE ANGEL NATHALIE

The image shifted. It showed Will reaching into the fridge, hands hovering over a big bar of chocolate, trying to decide between that and the large éclair next to it. He ignored the little medicine bottle in the side shelf of the fridge, even though it had his name printed there. He had never liked that bottle, he had never liked the needles.

I did everything f—

—or him! I gave up half my life for him!" Suzanne mumbled the words. King began to whine softly at her feet.

Outside, a car pulled up in the street, but no one in the room paid any attention to the red and blue lights flashing in through the window.

«« — »»

Gravity clutched at Nathalie, and she began to fall.

Jason clung on to her tight, and screamed in her ears, loud over the rushing wind.

"It's not quite flying, I'll admit!" he was yelling. "But sometimes I do this, just to remember how it used to feel!"

The city was spread below them, a million yellow lights twinkling in the darkness.

Nathalie could not tell how high or far Jason had taken them when he had forced her to dissipate. She recognized the curve of the river far below, saw the reaching fingers of London's modest skyscrapers heaving up out of the earth towards them.

She tried to force her flesh to shimmy back into the darkness, tried to pull herself back through the blackness that gaped the thickness of a shadow away, so that she could slide out again, back to the street, back to the house, back to Laura…

But Jason held her tight as they fell. He was blocking her, somehow. He would not let her vanish.

She set her teeth, and jerked, and together, their two bodies began to whirl wildly as they fell. The pillars of London reached up to meet them…

《《——》》

He never liked the needles, Laura said, and she showed her mother how hard she had tried to make him understand. Suzanne had never really cared. Suzanne had been too busy getting her hair done or shopping for shoes or going out for drinks with Max or with her friends.

You never cared, so I was the one who had to, Laura went on. It was the eternal struggle, twice a day.

In the morning, Laura would get both the needles ready, drawing the medicine up out of the bottle, and keeping them in the fridge. She tried to teach Will how to do it for himself, tried to show him what he needed to do.

She would sit and make Will inject himself while she watched.

He would never do it if she was not there.

Which meant she could never have much of a life herself.

I told you to make sure, she told her mother.

"He said he was doi—

—*ing it!* Suzanne thought back, but the thought was awash with guilt, and Laura ignored it.

Instead she pulled in an image she had never seen, but one she had imagined a thousand times, so clear it could have been real, so clear she was sure it was what had happened. She spun the fantasy in her head again. She turned it faster and faster, until it was spinning so fast there was no chance of it stopping. Then she lifted it clear and placed it in the centre of her mother's mind.

Suzanne had no choice but to watch.

Will was in his room. He was panting, he was sweating, his vomit cloaked the floor.

A single needle was on the table. Will had got it out of the fridge, after the first two days had gone by, when he had begun to realise that something was going wrong, that something in him was sick.

But he did not know if he should use it.

His sister had always got them ready for him.

She had told him it was almost as dangerous to have too much as it was to have too little.

What if this was too much?

Maybe that was why he felt so sick?

Maybe his mother had given him too much. He didn't think she had taken the right number of units into the needle when she had injected him before she had left, the morning before last.

What if she had given him too much?

His stomach heaved. He needed to piss again. Why did he keep needing to piss? He must have emptied half of himself down the toilet. He was so thirsty, but he didn't have the energy to move.

He cried and looked at the needle again. He wished his sister was here.

Why had she gone away?

"Don't worry, mum'll look after you," she had told him.

She had tried to be nice, but he knew she was angry with him, knew she wanted more than anything to get away from him.

People said he was stupid, but he knew that much.

He moaned softly to himself as his bladder emptied down his legs. He couldn't hold it in anymore.

He felt so tired.

Maybe if he just went to sleep, he would wake up and Laura would be back. She would clean him up and then they would sing songs together and go for a walk.

Part of him knew he shouldn't go to sleep. Part of him knew he had to get help.

But the floor seemed too comfortable…

Maybe he would just rest for a moment…

He stopped struggling.

His eyes flickered and closed.

His chest rose and fell, rose and fell, quick, quick, quick.

His last thought before he drifted away into the darkness was of how nice it would be to see his sister's face when she got back from her holiday.

When two days had passed without being able to get an answer from the house, Laura had persuaded Blake to drive them home early. She had called the police on the way.

By the time she arrived, the door had been broken down, and the paramedics were carrying Will out into the street. His face looked so thin and blank. His chest rose and fell like bellows. His breath smelt very sweet.

The worst thing was the look in their eyes.

"That's why he needs his insulin," they told her, severely, as if it had been her fault.

"When did he last have it?" They asked her, but of course, she did not know.

Her mother was supposed to have been there.

She had *promised*.

Laura rode in the ambulance. She had pretended not to recognise Suzanne as Max's car rolled into the street, pulling to one side to let the ambulance blue-light past.

Later, in the hospital, they had explained it all to her, while Will lay on the bed and his muscles twitched and his chest rose and fell.

They had explained about the acid in his blood and the lack of oxygen. They had explained about the movement that was left in his eyes, and how little that really meant. She asked what hope there was for recovery, and did not miss the way their eyes shifted as they told her they could not say.

And now she was alone. Now her brother was nothing but a lump of flesh in a hospital bed.

Why had her mother not been there?

Why had *no one* been there?

"It wasn't my—

—*fault*!" screamed Suzanne, and Laura realized all at once that she was screaming, too.

«««—»»»

They floated in silence, Jason and Nathalie, they fell towards the earth, as they had each fallen once before. Everything seemed to slow. In the dark reflected glass of the skyscraper by their side, Nathalie watched as their tumbling images swam closer and closer…

They smashed into the glass, just as she had hoped they would.

Nathalie punched a hand into a glass window as it flashed past. The impact separated them.

Their bodies tore apart. Jason glanced off and span down towards the river.

Nathalie bounced away from the building and out into clear space.

He was no longer touching her.

She concentrated. The ground rushed up to meet her.

Seething tendrils of blackness wrapped around her flesh.

«« —»»

Laura pulled away. The awareness of the broken landscape of her mother's mind crashed into nothing around her, and the room melted back into view.

Suzanne was curled up in the bed, shaking gently and quietly breaking apart.

Laura did not smile.

It wasn't happiness she felt.

But there was something else. Something was almost complete.

"Laura?" Max asked softly, stirring out of sleep.

Laura glanced at him.

"Hi, Max," she said flatly. "I was just leaving."

She looked around the room one last time.

«« —»»

The world seethed around Nathalie, and all at once she was shooting out of the darkness on a certain street by a certain door while the rain fell all around.

She had been falling very fast, and the road cracked and rippled around her as she slammed into the earth.

The two policemen were thrown up into the air, hit the ground in boneless heaps, and went sliding away across the wet floor.

Nathalie straightened up. She turned to the door, already coming up at a run...

...And Jason was there waiting for her.

He pushed the door open.

"Ladies first," said Jason, and followed her up the stairs.

«««—»»»

Laura opened her mind.

She spread it out before her closed eyes, a thousand thousand thousand things, every inch and moment of her, every sparkling thought and memory and fear.

It rippled and faltered.

This was everything she was. This was the sum of her.

It was time to go.

There was a pounding on the stairs.

A moment later, Nathalie was in the room. She thought she saw someone coming up behind her, but she was not certain, and really, she hardly cared.

"Laura," said Nathalie, the faintest touch of horror entering her voice as she began to reach out with her mind, as she began to realise instinctively what Laura was planning to do.

"I'll not be chosen by you, or anyone," she said. "It's my life. I will choose."

The last external impression her senses brought her was of the terrible look of loss on Nathalie's face.

Then Laura turned her thoughts inwards, and shut off the world outside.

She had been a quick study. Nathalie herself had told her that.

She wondered if even Nathalie had realized how well she had learnt.

She opened her mind wide, pulled it as spread and gaping as

it would go, until everything was there before her, all at once and together, encircled in the circumference of her thoughts.

Then she sparked a burning pillar out of the darkness, the same kind that Nathalie had tried to use on her earlier. It seemed so simple. Such a little trick. How had she never known it before?

She smiled in the darkened room, and a single tear-drop rolled behind her closed eye.

Then she turned the pillar inward, and put all her mind to flame.

«« —»»

"Hi Laura, this is Blake.

"I don't know where you are or what you're doing. I'm just phoning to say hi, and to try and find out where you are.

"Anyway…give me a call when you get this. See you soon, I guess.

"I love you. Bye."

«« —»»

Nathalie surged forward, but it was already too late.

She felt the ripple of her seared mind roll out from the girl on the bed.

The heat of it was terrible; and when it was gone, Laura was gone, too.

Nathalie reached for her, desperately pressed her mind against the girl she had tried to save.

Her breathing was steady, and her face was soft and gentle.

But her mind was no longer there. It had been burnt all away.

The room was silent and still.

Nathalie gradually became aware of the woman curled up in the bed. Her hair was peroxide blond, and her shoulders were shaking as she cried.

It was Laura's mother.

Nathalie felt the world lurch around her.

Something shifted, deep within.

She had tried. She had tried so hard.

But however hard she tried, people always let her down.

How much pain had been caused by this pathetic creature, crying and broken on the bed?

How much good, how much potential there had been in her daughter…and now that was burnt to ash and blown away.

She felt so tired.

She was always trying to save people who would not save themselves.

Slowly, she walked forward until she was standing over the weeping woman.

The woman shifted. She felt the presence leaning over her. She turned her head, and looked up at Nathalie.

"What…what's wrong with your eyes?" she asked Nathalie, tears staining her cheeks where her mascara had run.

Nathalie tilted her head.

"Nothing's wrong with them," she said. "Nothing at all."

Then she reached out a languid hand and snapped the woman's neck.

She fell back onto the bed. Her foot twitched a few times then stilled.

Nathalie turned to the man who was struggling up from the sheets, shrieking for help, reaching for something to use as a weapon.

She picked him up as easy as if he were a babe and hurled him towards the wall.

His body tore through the wall and blew it to pieces—plaster and bone and wood and strings of blood sailing out into the street beyond, mixing with the rain and the darkness.

She turned and looked at the dog.

The dog looked up at her, and whined.

She considered it for a moment.

Then she reached down and scratched it behind the ears.

"Good boy," she said.

There was a cough from a corner of the room.

"Well that was…not quite what I was expecting," admitted Jason. "I thought you were going to let them off with a caution."

"I did not do anything that wasn't deserved," said Nathalie, and her voice was low and hoarse.

Jason made a little tutting noise.

"You should know the rules by now, Nathalie. We're not allowed to do what you just did. You can give them enough rope to hang themselves; you can't string them up yourself."

Nathalie smiled, and Jason noticed her eyes for the first time.

"I told you, didn't I?" she said. "I'm not what you are. I'm something else."

She looked at him with eyes as perfect black as midnight. They seemed to suck all the light out of the room. Not a trace of yellow remained.

"You will fear me before I am done," she told him.

She took in the room one last time, the blood, and the plaster, and the girl on the bed, silent and peaceful and quite, quite still.

Then she wrapped her alabaster arms around the slightness of her frame, and called the darkness to her, tendrils of night leeching her in shadows and carrying her further from the light.

Part Three

The man in the red jumpsuit peered out of his one good eye. A scarlet rivulet ran away from him and off between chinks in the cobblestones. The stone felt cold and rough against his cheek. He welcomed the cold. It felt like half his face was on fire.

"So are you gonna get up?" a voice shouted down at him. It sounded close and a million miles away at the same time.

The man in the red jumpsuit stayed very still.

"What's that?" came the voice again. "I can't hear you, pussy! You still have a problem with the way we do things around here?"

The man in the jumpsuit opened his mouth to reply, but his tongue and half his face had swollen up, and it felt as if his mouth was full of grit.

"Huh?" came the taunting voice again. "What you say?"

There was the sound of feet coming closer, and he tensed his body just in time.

A boot was driven in under his ribcage, hard. He thought he felt something snap.

The man in the jumpsuit coughed involuntarily, and a globule of blood-stained phlegm came up.

A month ago, when he had first got here, he might have tried calling for help. He might even have thought of calling for one of the guards.

But that was a month ago. He had learnt quickly.

"I don't have a problem with you," he forced out quickly.

He sensed the man standing over him stop in the act of preparing another kick.

"What?" said the man with the hard boots. "Did you just say that you were a ball-kissing homo? I think that's what you said, just you didn't say it all that loud. Why don't you say it again, so all these gentlemen can hear?"

The man in the red jumpsuit didn't even pause to nod.

"I'm a ball-kissing homo," he said. He made his voice as loud and clear as he could, and there was a wave of laughter from the ring of other inmates that surrounded him. Not that they were all against him, not exactly. It's just, they weren't with him, either; and entertainment was thin enough round here that it was always easy for someone like Kain to get a cheap laugh. Mostly, the other guys were probably laughing because it wasn't them on the floor.

"Damn right you are," Kain muttered. He turned on his heel and walked away. "And stay the hell out of my business from now on."

The man in the red jumpsuit felt his body sag with relief. Nevertheless, he was careful to keep his face on the floor until the heavy footsteps had died away.

After that, it was business as normal. He felt more than saw the little group that had gathered around the disturbance begin to disperse. No one else kicked him, but no one else acknowledged him, either.

Except for Ray, of course.

Ray was his cellmate, he wasn't his friend. But Ray was small and weak, and in the first week of his stay—of what was meant to be a *long* stay—the man in the red jumpsuit had stood up for the smaller man.

I wouldn't do that now, the man in the red jumpsuit thought to himself. It was true: by now he had learnt that it didn't pay to go fighting other people's battles for them. It just made you a target yourself. Shit, who knew? If it wasn't for that, maybe Kain wouldn't be giving him such a hard time now. He had certainly marked himself out as a...as a what? A soft touch?

But then I wouldn't have anyone to help me up again after every beating, he thought as Ray shook his shoulder vaguely and asked if he was OK.

Would that be better, or worse?

He wasn't sure anymore, and that made him feel broken, somewhere deep down inside.

One month inside, and already he had decided that friends were liabilities. Shit, what was wrong with him?

But no, he realized, *it was before I ended up in here that I realized friends were liabilities.*

He sighed and let Ray drag him to his feet, and just for one moment while he let his guard down, he saw her face flash in front of his eyes.

She had been a liability.

And that was before he had been given this nice red jumpsuit and three square meals a day, courtesy of Her Majesty's pleasure.

No, he told himself firmly, and blocked her image from his mind.

"You OK?" Ray was saying, his breath stinking of cheap tobacco, his skinny fingers digging into his ribs as the smaller man tried to help him to his feet.

"I'm fine," mumbled the man in the red jumpsuit, but his face was already swollen up from the punches, and it came out as, "Um faghh."

"No you're not, you need to get to the infirmary, go see the doctor," Ray persisted.

The man in the red jumpsuit shook his head firmly. Whatever he was doing now, it was not waiting in line for two hours to see some joke of a doctor who told him his ribs were broken and his face was bruised, and that he was very sorry but he couldn't give him any pain relief stronger than Tylenol on account of the high probability that they would end up stolen or sold to some other inmate.

"I'm fine," he said again, more firmly, shaking Ray's hand off. "Just leave me alone, OK?"

He turned on his heel and strode away. Ray called something after him but he kept his head down and didn't answer.

He sensed a few other inmates giving him appraising looks, taking in his bruised face, but he ignored them and just walked faster. He made his way past a guard and back inside the main building where the inmates slept. The guard saw his face, but didn't say anything.

Easier for both of us that way, the man in the red jumpsuit thought; and though it was true, he couldn't help feeling bitter.

He had never been very good at looking the other way. That was one of his problems, he supposed. Except that one time…if he had only not looked the other way when she had gone running off, if only he had made more of an effort to find her…

But he cut the thought off before he could complete it.

She was gone, and he was alone, and if it was anyone's fault it wasn't his.

It was not his fault, and it wasn't Laura's either.

In fact, there was only one person whom he thought could reasonably take responsibility for what had happened, and the man in the red jumpsuit had absolutely no idea where she was right now.

And even if he did know, Nathalie wasn't even human.

He had to pass three more guards and undergo an extensive frisking before he was back at his cell. Ray was still outside in the courtyard, of course, but the cell wasn't empty.

A man in a well-tailored suit and dark glasses was slouched on the lower bunk, grinning at him with a mouth full of perfect white teeth.

The man in the red jumpsuit sighed. After everything that had happened today, he should have known he could expect another visit before he managed to get some sleep.

He walked into the cell and slouched down against one wall.

"Hello, Jason," he said neutrally to the figure.

The man in the suit took off his sunglasses to reveal poisonous yellow eyes, and cranked his smile up a notch.

"Hello, Blake," he said in a friendly tone. "Have you thought any more about my offer of supplying you with weapons or narcotics?"

Blake snorted, and reached into his pocket for a box of cigarettes. He hadn't smoked on the outside, not since he was fifteen, but he had made up his mind to start again pretty much as soon as the judge's gavel had fallen. After all, it wasn't likely that he'd be enjoying a ripe old age on the outside. Two murders had been laid at his door, and that wasn't mentioning whatever had been done to Laura. They couldn't think of any charge to level against him with regards to Laura, but the prosecution had made certain everyone knew exactly what state Laura was in when they had found her.

If only he hadn't gone there. If only he had waited at the apartment, like he had originally planned. If only he hadn't got there before the police, just in time to be seen...

"Hey, kid, I'm talking to you," said Jason, not unkindly, and Blake was snapped out of his reverie.

"What?" shouted Blake. He glared at the daemon. "Why have you come here again? I've already told you, I don't want anything you can offer me. Why can't you just write me off as a dead cause, and leave me the hell alone?"

"Oooh," mocked the daemon, "someone's touchy today."

"What, are you a *gay* daemon now?" asked Blake.

"I'll have you know I'm all for equal rights," said Jason archly. "I don't like the tone you're taking with me. It's rude, obnoxious, and borderline homophobic." He leaned closer and lowered his voice. "I mean, FYI, I haven't had a penis for at least two thousand years, and even when I did I was strictly interested in the ladies. But still. This is the twenty-first century. You have to be careful what you say."

Blake shook his head and exhaled a cloud of foul-smelling smoke. The only cigarettes he could afford here were cheap foreign rubbish.

"Whatever," he said. "I'm not interested. Got it?"

Jason sat up slowly on the bed and rubbed one hand down his smooth-shaven cheeks.

"Ah, fair enough. I just thought you might have changed your mind after the beating you just received. You sure I can't interest you in one of these?"

He opened one side of his jacket, to reveal a wide selection of small but efficient looking knives, pistols, garrotting wires, and other ephemera of death.

"I'm not making a deal with you," said Blake flatly. "I know what you are, remember? Even if I didn't know anything about you, the very fact that I know you exist means that my, ah, *immortal soul*, must be worth something, right? And anyway," he added, "I *do* know you."

"And what's that supposed to mean?" said Jason, in mock outrage. "I'm just doing my job. Why do you always feel the need to get *personal*? It's just so hurtful."

Blake stayed silent. Jason got up, sidled over to where Blake was leaning against the wall, and slid down next to him.

"Look, I'm not going to pretend that it was chance that I decided to take you on as a client..." Jason said.

"I don't *want* to be your client!" interrupted Blake.

"That's not your choice," continued Jason smoothly, "when it comes to temptation, it's something of a free market. And since we had already been introduced through our, ah, mutual friend, it means I'm just at much greater liberty to be open about what I'm offering." He grinned widely. "It's such a pain, you know, having to whisper in ears, leave little tempting objects around, that sort of thing. It's so nice being able to offer you guns and shit straight up, even if you do always turn me down."

Blake shook his head and looked away.

"She's not my friend," he said after a moment. "If she was my friend, she wouldn't have killed my best friend, her mother, and her stepdad."

"Well, you're forgetting the part where she left you to rot in this cell for her crimes, while she went gallivanting off into the night," said Jason, "but essentially you're right. Point taken. But that doesn't change the fact that I come here as much to get away from the tedious business of subtle manipulations that sometimes take years to bear fruit." Jason paused, and tilted his head to one side. "Anyway. Enough about me. How are you?"

Blake glared at the daemon.

"You really are a dick, aren't you?" he said at length.

Jason gave a little sheepish grin and raised his hands.

"What can I say? I'm a *daemon*. It's sort of in the job description."

"Just leave me alone," said Blake. He stubbed the cigarette out on the wall, and walked over to the bed. He lay down, and put one arm over his eyes, cutting out the dreary prison light.

The room was silent. Just as Blake was beginning to hope that Jason had gone, the daemon spoke again.

"You know, it really was a shame about Laura," he said softly. "She was such a talented girl. Damaged, of course. But talented. But then, I suppose that was why she chose to kill herself…"

Blake didn't even realise he was getting up, but he was suddenly standing close to Jason, his fists curled around those finely tailored lapels, his face pressed up against those daemonic yellow eyes.

"Laura. Did not. Kill herself." He said the words softly, but with great force. "She did not commit suicide. Nathalie killed her. It was *her* fault." He faltered for a moment, and let go of Jason. "And it was my fault, too. I knew there was something… dark there. Something that we should have stayed away from. Something I should have kept Laura away from."

Jason was looking at him with a vague expression of admiration.

"Well, little man, I never thought you had it in you," he said after a moment, sounding vaguely impressed. "Of course, I'm tempted to teleport a few dozen scorpions into your bowels. But nevertheless. I'm impressed."

Blake shrugged.

"Go on then," he said. "It's not as if the food here's any good."

Jason clicked his teeth a few times.

"Ah, maybe some other time," he said. "Now I am quite sure I saw some very authentic rage in your eyes there—are you *quite* sure about the guns?"

"Yes," said Blake. "Quite."

"Well then, if I can't offer you a weapon, then how about…" his voice cut off abruptly.

Blake shivered. The fillings in his teeth suddenly hurt. The feeling passed in an instant, and when it had gone, Jason's face was changed. The mocking smile was gone.

"Hah," said Jason a moment later. His voice sounded different. "Well, it seems I must cut this little visit short. Funnily enough, I have just received a message regarding our mutual friend."

Blake stayed silent. There was something different about Jason. He looked…Blake struggled to put his finger on it…

That was it.

He looked *worried*.

Wondering if he was really saying it, Blake found himself asking, "Is everything OK?"

Jason shrugged, and tried to force something of his usual smug confidence back into his voice.

"Sort of," he said shortly. "But no one likes getting called to see the boss, do they?"

He shook himself and took a deep breath.

"Well, so long," said Jason, flashing Blake a last smile. "Have a think about what I said. I'll be waiting for you when you change your mind."

Then he tipped him a wink and casually vanished into a puff of seething black vapor.

"I won't," said Blake softly.

But he was thinking about the way Laura looked the last time he had seen her. The daemon had done a good job of getting to him. However deep he tried to bury the things that had happened to him, to forget what that…that *creature* that called herself Nathalie had done to them, it was not buried deep enough to stop

Jason digging it up. And now Jason was getting called to see "the boss"—whoever *that* was—about something related to Nathalie.

He closed his eyes and tried to sleep, but sleep didn't come for hours.

Sometimes, a person is too angry to sleep.

«««—»»»

Ben Prichard was half-asleep when he heard his father get back, but the sound of the door slamming woke him up, and he had made sure the rolling pin was in his hand when he had let his eyes close earlier that night.

The selection of his weapons had bothered him: which to choose? There were plenty of knives in the house, but Jesus, he wasn't a killer. He just wanted to show his old man that someone was ready to stand up to him, that he couldn't get away with this shit anymore. After all, he would be twelve next month. Almost a man. This was the fourth night this week that Ben's father hadn't come home from work. Which meant he had gone straight out to get drunk. Not that there were all that many drinking holes in a town the size of Clifton, Colorado—population 1,769, thank you for visiting, and please drive carefully—but David Prichard was well known in all of them. And if he had been drinking again tonight, his father would likely be in another of his mean moods when he got back. Usually, Ben was spared the brunt of those bad moods—as long as he stayed in his room, and kept quiet, that was.

But it was difficult to keep quiet. It was difficult not to listen, when you heard the shouts and the protests, when you heard the sound of a fist striking flesh, and felt the vibrations through the floorboards as a body hit the ground.

Three nights this week he had lain awake and told himself that he was a coward, and hated himself for not getting up, not going to confront his father, even if he knew the attempt would likely be futile. Three mornings this week, he had risen late to find that his father had left for work, and that his mother had a new shade of angry purple blossoming on her face. He had stayed home from school, telling his mother that he had the runs, though really, of course, it was so he could look after her.

But this morning he had decided. Enough was enough.

He wasn't going to be a coward anymore. That's why he had stayed up with the TV on, instead of going to bed around the time his mother did.

He hadn't meant to sleep for long, and he had been sure that he would wake on his own and pussy out before his father got back.

Oops.

It looked like pussying out might not be an option, after all.

He looked at the rolling pin and licked his lips. His hand looked awfully small next to that chunky slab of wood. But he had practiced swinging the thing earlier that day, when he was choosing what would make an effective—but non-lethal—weapon, and he was fairly certain he could hit hard enough with it to have the desired effect.

Next door, in the hall, he heard his father's heavy footsteps, then heard him curse loudly as he stumbled against one of the walls.

At least he's drunk, Ben tried to tell himself. *If I can just keep my head, maybe I can dodge out of his way. I don't need to get more than a few shots in. Just enough to make my point.*

That's what he told himself, but he didn't take much comfort in it, not really.

After all, his father was in his forties and weighed just shy of 250 pounds. While Ben was eleven and weighed…well, he wasn't a heavily-built boy.

That doesn't matter, he told himself. *I've already decided. No backing down. It doesn't matter if he beats the shit out of me. He has to know that someone's ready to stand up to him. He has to learn that…*

There were two more steps, and then suddenly the handle to the living room door was turning.

This was it. Sink or swim.

The door opened wide, and David Prichard was standing there, peering into the gloom of the room.

"What the hell?" he asked to the room at large. "Where's my Goddamn dinner? Why's the TV on?"

Then he stopped, because he realized suddenly that it wasn't his wife standing there in the darkness, but his son.

"Ben?" he asked, then belched loudly.

Ben could smell the sour, beer-and-peanuts odor from across the room. It made him want to be sick.

He took a deep breath and stepped forward.

"Yeah dad, it's me," he said, trying to make his voice sound deep, but it came out in a rasp anyway.

"What're you doing up?" asked his father. "And where's your mother?"

"Dad," Ben went on, forcing himself to take another step, "this has to stop. This isn't right, the way you're treating her, the way you…"

But Ben's dad wasn't listening to him. He was laughing. Suddenly, it seemed, the sight of his son looking all serious and trying to have a man-to-man conversation with him was too much.

"That's not *right*?" his father repeated, holding his shaking belly, and taking his baseball cap off to wipe the sweat from his brow. "This has got to *stop*? Well, hell, boy, when did you grow such big balls? Last time I looked you were still playing at painting up your little army toys. Guess I haven't been paying that much attention, didn't notice when my own boy decided to grow up and become a man on me."

He laughed harder, and leant his head in the palm of one sweaty hand.

Ben tried to force himself to go on, but he knew he was losing his nerve. So he didn't say anything. Instead, he took another step towards his father. He even raised his weapon uncertainly. Only a few inches up, but that was the most he could manage right then.

David Prichard looked at him. His grin stayed where it was, but he stopped laughing.

111

"And what's this, boy?" he asked. His voice was softer now, more dangerous.

"Dad," Ben tried again, though his legs felt like water, and his voice sounded high and thin. "I've decided, I'm going to stand up to…"

"You're going to stand up to me?" his father interrupted. "Well isn't that heroic. Go on then, you little fuck."

His father straightened up and puffed out his chest. He spread his arms wide and took a step closer to Ben. Ben moved backwards, but his father came forward again.

"Go on then, I said," his father repeated. "If you're a man, prove it! Show me what you've got. Hit me."

Ben tried to look his father in the eye, but he couldn't. He just couldn't. His eyes slid down to the floor, his shoulders sagged.

"That's what I thought," his father said quietly.

He leaned in close. His breath really was awful.

For a moment, Ben thought he was in for the beating of his life.

But then his father was drawing back. He was walking out of the room, heading towards the stairs.

"Put something in the oven for me, then get to bed," his father ordered. "I'm going to see your mother, *boy*. Just so you know, next time you decide you're a man, you better sure as hell have the balls to back yourself up. I don't let anyone talk shit like that to me. Don't think I'll go easy on you just 'cos you're a kid. Not 'cos you're *my* kid, either."

Then he was climbing the stairs, and Ben was alone in the dark room.

A few moments later, he heard noises from upstairs. Then he began to cry.

He carried the rolling pin back into the kitchen, and hung it back up next to the knives.

Damn it, why couldn't he do it?

He was weaker than his father, of course he was. But he hadn't even *tried*. That was what made it hurt so much. His father was right.

He didn't even have the balls to try.

Numbly, he pulled a pizza out of the freezer and threw it into the oven. The noises from upstairs were getting louder. Ben shut his eyes for a few moments.

Just go to bed, he told himself.

He left the kitchen light on, and started climbing the stairs.

He was halfway up when he heard the knocking at the door.

For a moment he froze.

Who could be knocking at this time? Surely no one he knew. Or no one with any good news.

And what if it was someone who wanted to speak to his parents?

What if they heard the sounds from upstairs?

Then it would be good! A part of himself screamed. But another part knew that it wouldn't be good, not good at all for whoever it was who was at the door. Then there might be a fight, a *real* fight, and who knew what might happen then. He looked uneasily at the knife rack. He, Ben, was no killer…but his father?

He knew for a fact his father had a .22 stashed in his room somewhere. He had even seen him pull it on someone, one of his mother's male friends, someone who had been coming round a little too often for David Prichard's liking a couple of years back.

No, it was better for everyone if he just forgot about the knocking on the door and went up to bed.

It was probably better if for now, he forgot about everything.

He took another step…at least, he meant to. But for some reason, his foot refused to move. It just stood there, as still as if it was frozen to the cheap, beer-stained carpet that lined the staircase.

The knocking came again, and with the knocking there came a…to call it a wind would be wrong, because it wasn't the air that was moving. It was something else, something deeper…

For a moment, Ben felt as if he was teetering on the edge of a vertiginous abyss, as if the world was shifting around him, and any second he was going to fall into…what?

And then the feeling was gone, and all at once he felt a warm, wonderful glow creeping up from the deepness of his stomach.

113

THE FALL OF THE ANGEL NATHALIE

It was if he had suddenly remembered it was Christmas tomorrow, a *real*, deep Christmas, not one designed by advertising companies to sell thousands of cheap plastic toys, but something more pure and wonderful than that.

Before he knew what he was doing, he was running down the stairs and flinging the door open wide.

It was a young woman, with long dark hair and dressed in simple, plain clothes.

She was smiling at him. Her eyes were as black as night. Even where they should be white, they were black.

"Hello," the woman said to him. "There is a problem here, I think. Can I come in? I promise I will make it better."

Her voice sounded strange to him. He couldn't quite place the accent, but he was sure it was from nowhere nearby.

Ben nodded mutely, and stood aside. He knew all at once and with complete confidence that the woman was right. She would make it all better.

He closed the door behind her, and then did not know what to do.

"My name's Ben," he said after a pause.

"I know," said the woman. "I am Nathalie. I'm new here. I needed to get away from where I was before. I needed a fresh start. What better place than a lovely little town like this?"

Ben swallowed.

"What do you…What do you do?" he asked her, though he thought he knew the answer already.

Nathalie smiled at him.

"Come with me," she said. "I'll show you."

She moved up the stairs. Her feet fell very softly. It was almost as if she were floating upwards, Ben thought.

Ben followed her, then stopped. He looked at the knife rack.

"Don't worry about that," said Nathalie, without turning around. "I'll show you much better things than knives and rolling pins."

And then she did.

There was a place of deep darkness, and Jason was falling deeper in. It would be inaccurate to say that this place was deep in the sense that it was actually, physically under the ground—although the entrances to it often started there—it was more of a…more of a state of mind.

Daemonhearth is one name for it, though there are others. Personally, Jason thought "Daemonhearth" sounded old-fashioned and rather pompous, but then, it wasn't his choice. The High Darkness had decided that the old name would stick, so the old name it was.

And now he was being summoned to see the High Darkness himself…

Oh dear.

He took a deep breath (not that there was any air down here), and tried to relax…and then he was there.

Twisted structures of rock and metal loomed above him, housing all sorts of chambers, dungeons, and private dwellings. Many of his colleagues elected to live down here, though frankly, Jason wasn't certain he saw the attraction. And the dungeons were not all that popular nowadays. Hundreds of years ago, when the human population was much smaller, and the number of claimed souls was proportionally smaller, too, many prestigious members of his race made a practice of keeping claimed souls down in those dungeons, fermenting them, refining them like fine wines. The thinking was that one could make the drink sweeter, more potent, if only the process of torment was allowed to continue after the physical death of the host body.

If there was one thing the average daemon wanted from his next meal, it was potency.

Nowadays, of course, supply was not really a problem. In the time it had taken Jason to travel from Blake's prison to this far corner of Daemonhearth, somewhere in the region of one hundred and fifty people had come into the world. Statistically, at least a half of them would end up on some daemon's platter.

115

THE FALL OF THE ANGEL NATHALIE

All this meant that the trend for torturing, tormenting, and otherwise refining the quality of claimed souls had rather died out, and as a consequence most of the many dungeons which festooned the caverns and endless, dim byways of this deep-buried world were entirely empty almost all of the time.

The High Darkness did not care about that, though.

Not that he was one for tradition, not exactly. He just *liked* torturing souls. And he wanted everyone who worked for him to know that.

Jason sighed and tried to pull himself together. He wiped one hand across his brow. Was he actually *sweating*? He tried to remember the last time that had happened. He thought it was probably around the time of the French Revolution.

Well.

It would not do to keep the High Darkness waiting.

Jason set off towards the large, plain door he knew was waiting for him in the cavern wall a few hundred yards away. It was forbidden to dissipate oneself within the confines of Daemonhearth, but then this never usually caused any major problems, because, of course, it did not really exist in the usual physical sense, and anyone entering it could pretty much choose where they wanted to manifest to the nearest inch or so.

If he had wanted to, Jason could have arrived standing next to his boss's door.

He just felt that he wanted the extra walking time to prepare.

The High Darkness wanted to see *him*.

When was the last time that had happened?

Not for many years. He had done quite a good job of blocking the whole experience out...

He arrived at the door.

It was large and awfully, crushingly plain.

There wasn't even a placard or number.

Anyone meaning to enter that door knew very well what they were getting themselves into.

He hesitated for a moment, then raised his hand to knock.

The door swung open on well-oiled hinges.

The room was brightly lit by clean, white electric bulbs. They glared down from several lights that were strung from the ceiling, none of which were plugged in, and they exposed every cowering inch of the stone floor.

Everything was very neat and tidy. There was a set of drawers, a medium-sized wooden desk, and behind the desk was a chair.

In the chair sat the High Darkness.

He was a little tall—slightly above average height, but only slightly—and rather thin. He had neatly combed grey-brown hair and meticulously clean fingernails. And his eyes…

…His eyes were blue.

There was no poisonous yellow, no deep darkness there.

Just dusky-blue eyes, the color of the clear sky an hour or so before sunset.

Oh yes, remembered Jason. *He wears contacts*.

"High Darkness," said Jason respectfully.

"Jason," said the creature that looked like an anaemic, middle-aged man. He smiled thinly. "Thank you for coming so promptly."

"Of course," said Jason. He made a point of staying standing until the High Darkness gestured casually to the seat across from the desk. Then he sat.

The High Darkness stared at him in silence.

After a moment, he said, "You know why I have summoned you here."

It wasn't a question, but Jason nodded.

"I have here a report filed by yourself regarding the actions of your…trophy," the High Darkness went on, in a low, soft voice. "Quite why it took so long to reach this desk, I do not know. You are aware, I am sure, that I am a very busy, ah, man. Nevertheless, some things are urgent, and some things are less so. And this," he held up the report Jason had filed a few months ago, a few days after he had last seen his one-time friend, "this… is *urgent*."

Jason cleared his throat and opened his mouth to speak.

117

"High Darkness," he began, but the High Darkness held up one finger, and the words choked in Jason's throat.

"Like I said, I am very busy," the High Darkness went on. "It will save time if I ask the questions and you answer them. Do you understand?"

Jason nodded, a little too quickly.

"Good," said the High Darkness. "So. You saw this Nathalie—an ex-angel whose fall you were personally responsible for—you actually *saw* her commit these acts?"

Jason nodded again.

"You can speak, you know," said the High Darkness, smiling his thin smile again. His blue eyes stared relentlessly.

"Yes," said Jason. "I was standing there. In the room, I was waiting for her. She killed them. She killed both of them. She broke the woman's neck, and she threw the man out of the building."

The High Darkness frowned.

"Was it a high building?" he asked. "Humans are frail creatures, but a fall from a first or second floor is not all that often fatal."

Jason shrugged.

"She didn't throw him through the window, she threw him through the wall."

"Ah yes, of course," said the High Darkness, looking back at the report in his hands, and leafing idly through it. "And you mention here, also, why she did this. Anger, hate, frustration, all our usual tools. I must say, it was a rather nasty little trick you played on her. In other circumstances, I might be congratulating you."

"Thank you," said Jason, flatly.

"In these circumstances, of course, I am not," continued the High Darkness. "What you do not mention, I think, is whether she understood the gravity of the acts she was committing? Not that that will make any difference in the end, naturally. A rabid dog *is* a rabid dog, after all. You may answer the question."

Jason hesitated.

"She…she must have known," he said at last. "She was an angel. She was a very powerful one. She knew all the rules, our side's and theirs'. She knew what was forbidden."

"Yes, yes she did," mused the High Darkness. "But looking back, it seems she never cared *too* carefully for what was forbidden, did she? After all, that was how you tempted her. That was how you claimed her."

"Yes," he agreed softly, looking at the spotless floor.

The High Darkness let the silence last for a few moments.

"Anyway," said the High Darkness at last, leaning back in his chair and looking away. "The facts of the matter are clear. The daemon known as Nathalie knowingly and without threat to her own person directly caused the death of two humans. In so doing, she broke the terms of the laws that bind us and protect us all. She has consumed the souls of two individuals by brute force. Wittingly or otherwise, she has poisoned herself. She…"

The High Darkness stopped mid-sentence and looked at Jason.

"You say she knew the laws very well," he said, "but do you think she knew *why* those laws are in place? Do you think she knows what is happening to her, now that she has consumed un-processed souls?"

Jason did not know, not for sure, but he shook his head.

If she had known what would happen to her, surely she would never have done it?

"I see," said the High Darkness. "Well, well. She will be in for a surprise then. If you do not find her before they begin in earnest, that is."

Jason frowned.

"I…You want me to find her?" he asked.

The High Darkness smiled his thin smile again.

"Of course you are to find her," replied the High Darkness. "After all, you were the one who drank her higher soul. You were the one who tempted her into calling the Hecatomb down on herself. You are linked to her. You will be linked to her forever. You can find her. And when you find her…you can destroy her."

Jason's head came up sharply.

"Destroy her?" he echoed. "You want me to…?"

"To destroy her, yes," the High Darkness said. "It's really very simple. Do you want me to explain it to you again? She broke the rules, she has poisoned herself and stolen from the communal cauldron, she would pay for this even if we did not punish her; but punish her we will, and most severely. Or rather, *you* will punish her. Do you understand me now, or do I need to cancel my entire schedule and walk you through it one more time?"

Jason closed his eyes, licked his lips, and opened them again.

"No, High Darkness," he said flatly. "I understand. Whatever you command, I will do. Only…only how am I meant to…"

"How are you meant to destroy her?" said the High Darkness, and he was smiling again, only this time the smile was not so thin. It even touched his eyes. "Do not worry about that. We have certain objects here for necessities such as this. The Higher Authorities have been diligent in ensuring we have the capacity to punish our transgressors just as they have the capacity to punish theirs. After all, we couldn't expect them to get their hands dirty with our little problems."

The High Darkness got to his feet and walked to where a small chest of drawers stood in one corner of the room. He opened the top drawer and took out a little black wooden box, of a kind that might be used to hold an expensive piece of jewellery. He handed it to Jason.

Jason fingered the black wood warily. It felt cold and heavy in his hands.

"Open it," said the High Darkness.

Jason licked his lips, and opened the box.

"Oh," he said.

He shut the box.

"Does it bring back memories?" asked the High Darkness.

Jason nodded.

"Then I do not need to warn you not to touch it," said the High Darkness, returning to his desk.

Jason hesitated.

"How do I…" he began to ask, but the High Darkness cut him off.

"I'm sure you have lots of clever little people in your pocket, Jason," he said. "Talk to one of them and…persuade them to help you."

The High Darkness moved slowly back around his desk and sat down.

"Find her," he said. "Find her, use the weapon I have given you, destroy her before she commits any more…infractions. Then bring me back the box, and we can both go about our business."

The High Darkness was already putting away the report Jason had filed, and pulling out another wad of papers. He was no longer looking at Jason.

"Yes, High Darkness," said Jason. He turned around and made for the door.

"I assume I do not need to tell you," said the High Darkness without looking up, "exactly what will happen to you if you fail me in this?"

Jason shook his head.

"Good," said the High Darkness. "I have no especial desire to consume your soul—what's left of it, at any rate—but do not doubt that if the occasion commands it, I would not hesitate for a second."

He looked up, and smiled thinly again.

"Who knows?" he went on. "I might even enjoy it."

Jason nodded, and waited to make sure the High Darkness was finished with him.

When he was sure that nothing more was forthcoming, he left the room quietly and closed the door behind him.

Destroy Nathalie?

He had thought his meeting with the High Darkness would be difficult, but this…

But then, maybe he *had* known where things were going. Wasn't that the way things were always heading?

There was something…uncompromising about her. There always had been. And to survive in this world, one thing you needed to be was flexible.

Look at him. He had fallen, true, and before Nathalie was even close. But he had *changed*. He had seen what was demanded of him, seen how he needed to adapt to fit into his new role…and he had adapted.

Not like Nathalie.

Poor, selfless, uncompromising, stupid Nathalie.

She hadn't been willing to play by the rules, and now…now he would have to be her executioner.

Not that he minded. Not that he felt that it was unfair, or foolish, or…or his fault.

She had known the rules. She had known the price of things.

And as the High Darkness had said, it wasn't that dissimilar than the way one would deal with a rabid dog.

But if only…

He stopped himself in mid thought. He couldn't allow himself to think these things.

He had been given a job to do. He would do it…or he would end up as dinner for a daemon so ancient he made Jason feel young again, something he hadn't really been for millennia.

So.

On to business.

He thought about the…weapon the High Darkness had given him.

Calling it a weapon was being generous. If it was a weapon, then it was practically the definition of a double-edged sword.

But the High Darkness had been right: he really did have a lot of clever little people in his pocket. The problem was, not just any clever person would do. This required some very specific skills…

Light dawned on his face.

The perfect name had just come to him. Of course, he would probably have to remind her of her obligations…But that was never a problem. In fact, he would probably enjoy it…

Jason made ready to leave Daemonhearth. But before he did so, he put the little black box in the deepest pocket he could find.

Sometimes, the deepest pocket is not deep enough.

Not deep enough by far.

«««—»»»

The street looked so clean. Ben couldn't remember it ever having been so clean before.

He was walking home from school—he hadn't had to take a day off to look after his mother for a while now—and even though he still couldn't get his head around long division, he was feeling good. *Really* good.

Partly it was the sunshine, partly it was the clean streets... but mostly it was that he knew he did not have to worry about that violent, drunk *bastard* that he had been unfortunate enough to have for a father ever again—

—*but did he deserve it?*—

The thought flashed through his mind, and Ben's footsteps faltered for a moment. He felt a sharp stab of something cold and awful rise up from the deepness of his belly, like cold vomit... but then it was as if something...*derailed*...in his head. It was if the thought had slammed straight into an icy, invisible barrier somewhere behind his eyes.

He shook his head and breathed deeply.

The thought subsided. He took another breath, looked around him, and carried on walking.

What had he been thinking?

He couldn't remember. He felt a vague uncomfortable feeling, like an itch at the back of his head that he couldn't quite reach.

He let it go. After all, what could possibly be the matter? It was such a beautiful day.

He could smell the cake before he opened the front door, and as soon as he stepped inside, the rich, warm scent enveloped him and drew him forward. There was another smell there too, of course: the smell of cigarettes, but that smell had been present in the house a lot lately, and Ben was quite used to it by now.

It was funny, he used to associate the smell of cigarette smoke with something bad. It was probably because his father—

—he's dead—

His father occasionally used to come back stinking of cigarettes, and that meant that he had gotten *really* drunk. Ben frowned again, minutely, and one of his eyebrows twitched.

"Hello, darling," said his mother brightly. She was washing up the bowls in which the cake that was cooking in the oven had been mixed. She looked so happy.

Almost as happy as me, Ben thought, and smiled back at her.

"Hello there Ben," said the other lady, the one smoking the cigarette. She looked at him with those huge, black eyes. Ben gazed back adoringly.

"Hello Nathalie," he replied, then looked shyly at his shoes.

"How was your day—"

"Have you had a good day at school-"

The two women asked their questions at the same time. Ben's mother hung her head demurely.

"I'm sorry," she said, but Nathalie brushed the apology aside with a languid hand.

"Never mind," she said. "I hope you're not too tired from school Ben? You remember that we have work to do?"

As a matter of fact, Ben *did* feel tired…but as soon as Nathalie said those words, it was as if a breeze had blown in from somewhere green and fresh, and all the cobwebs were brushed away.

"I feel fine," he told her.

"Good," said Nathalie, stubbing out the cigarette and jumping up from the cabinet she had been leaning against. "Now did you do what I asked today?"

Oh, yeah.

That was funny, he'd completely forgotten about the little mission she had given him. Not forgotten to *do* it, of course. He didn't think he would *ever* forget to do something she asked of him, not ever. He wasn't sure he would be able to disobey her. Even thinking about it made him feel giddy.

No, he had done what she had asked of him, then forgotten about it until just now, until exactly the moment she asked him about it.

That was strange.

"No, I did it," he told her. "I did it to all of them, exactly like you told me."

Nathalie smiled at him. She looked very beautiful when she smiled.

"Let's sit down in the other room, and you can tell me about it," she said. "Let's give your mother some peace."

They went through into the living room. Ben glanced through the glass double doors that opened out into the back yard. Some of the branches of the apple tree outside were twisted and broken and—

—and that's where he fell, when he jumped out the window. The sound of branches/bones cracking and then when he tried to get up when he tried to get up and she followed him down and her hands looked so pale in the moonlight, thin and pale...but strong, too—

And Ben looked away for a moment and had to sit down because he felt dizzy.

Nathalie saw where he had been looking. She walked over and closed the curtains, blocking out the view of the garden and darkening the room.

"That's better," she told him, and she was right. Ben did feel better. Actually, he felt great. What had he been worrying about? He couldn't remember.

"Now," said Nathalie, "show me how you did it. Imagine I was one of them, and do it to me."

Ben took a deep breath. He concentrated.

He looked into Nathalie's eyes. It was like staring into the dark patches between the stars on a clear night.

He reached out for her, and there she was.

He felt her mind. It burned in front of him, glowing and rippling, a vast ocean of fire.

It was so different from all the others, from the others he had felt today.

Most of the others were so…so *small*, so *simple* by comparison. And so unguarded.

He had been able to slip inside them with ease. Well, most of them. A few were slightly more complex…and he had even felt one or two probing back towards him, as if his own prying had awoken something deeply buried, something that they hadn't even known they possessed…

"Which ones?" asked Nathalie quickly, and Ben felt dizzy again, because he wasn't sure if he had been speaking his thoughts aloud, explaining things to Nathalie…or come to that, if she had even spoken to him in words, or in something…deeper.

He took a breath to steady himself.

Then he told her which minds had felt him exploring them, and which had attempted to put up some form of rudimentary defence.

When she asked him what he had done to those minds, he answered her without question.

She smiled at him. "You know," she said, "you make a much better pupil than others I have had in the past. You are so much more willing to do the things that need to be done. I think I made the right choice with you. Some things are better not left to chance."

Ben thought about this for a moment.

"I'm not sure I was able to do it to the others as well as you did it to me," he said. "Miss Marston—she's the Math teacher— she was difficult. I think she realized what I was doing, right at the last moment. She tried to…to block me, somehow. So I pushed harder and well…I think maybe I pushed a little too hard in the end."

He remembered the sensation. It was like the smell of something greasy burning, only it was in his head, and he knew it was coming from Miss Marston.

"What happened to her?" asked Nathalie.

"She said she had to leave early," replied Ben. "She said she had a headache, but I saw her eyes, and there was something wrong with them. Her left one kept looking sideways. I don't think she could move it anymore." He thought for a moment. "Was that OK? Did I hurt her?"

He hoped he hadn't hurt her. He had always liked Miss Marston, who was young and pretty, and sometimes brought in little cupcakes that she baked herself when it was the last day of term.

Nathalie smiled at him, and there was something sad in her eyes.

"Oh, you are so sweet to worry about her," she told him. "But what you have to remember, Ben, is that you have to put these little things in perspective. It is possible you have hurt her. But then, in the long run, things will be better for it. Trust me. You will see."

Ben looked at her doubtfully.

"Will it make you feel better if I promise to go and see Miss Marston first this evening?" she asked him. "You've done well, and I think I'll be busy tonight. But I can see Miss Marston first, if you want. By the sound of things, she seems like exactly the sort of person we are looking for. We do want our town to be *strong*, after all, don't we?"

Ben bit his lip.

He was sure that Nathalie was right, it was just…

It was just that horrible *burning* smell.

Nathalie sat down next to him, and brushed his cheek gently with one of her pale hands.

Her skin felt soft. Soft, and very cold…and underneath that, her hand felt strong.

"You're only young," she told him. "You're young, but you've seen how bad things can get. I don't need to tell you that the world can be a terrible place. Filled with terrible people."

"I know, but…" Ben began.

"Like I said," interrupted Nathalie, "you know very well how bad things can be. Even if you do need a prod to remember that now. It's very difficult to make a difference in a world that's full of evil. More difficult than you can possibly imagine; too difficult…unless you allow yourself to get your hands dirty once in a while. So I am starting right here."

She touched Ben softly on the chest, just below his heart.

"I am starting with you, with this town," she continued. "And the first thing we need to do to make this town wholesome—and to make sure it *stays* wholesome—is to find the people who are too far gone to be saved and to…get rid of them. After that, the next step is to find anyone who has the potential to help, and make sure that potential is awoken. Which is what you have been helping me to achieve," she added, getting up and smiling at him. "You are very helpful to me, Ben. I don't want you to forget that."

Ben felt as if his heart would burst. He felt so happy, so proud.

Nathalie reached the door, and turned to him once more.

"Now go and eat your dinner," she told him with mock-sternness. "After all, we need to keep you strong. There's still an awful lot of people in this town, and I can't test them all on my own."

Ben nodded. Now that she mentioned it, he could feel his tummy rumbling angrily. When was the last time he had eaten?

"What about you?" he asked. "Aren't you hungry? Don't you want to eat with us?"

Nathalie tilted her head slightly to one side. Her black eyes glinted.

"Don't worry about me," she told him. "I've been eating very well since I came to this town. I'm sure I'll find something very filling for dinner."

«««—»»»

She placed the eye back into the socket, and held her needle up to the light. The little girl cried harder, but June's gaze didn't flicker.

"Hush, my darling," she said in her hoarse voice. "Just stay very still, and it won't hurt a bit."

"Just stay still," the little girl echoed, trying to sound brave, but her voice shook.

June held the needle steady for a moment longer, then with a jerk she plunged it down.

The little girl gasped.

June's hand moved up and down in a blur. Her movements were tiny and precise.

No one in the room breathed.

"There!" said June a moment later, biting through the thin cotton strand with her teeth, and holding the doll up to the light for the little girl and her mother to admire. "As good as new!"

Her voice was very deep and ragged. It always had been.

That, combined with the way she looked, always frightened children. Frightened them at first, anyway; but as soon as they stepped into her shop, or took their beloved doll into her work-room (or their broken model train, for that matter; she did not just specialise in toys for girls) the children forgot all about the way June looked, or the strange way she walked, or the guttural drawl of her voice.

How could they stay scared of her, when she made such wonderful toys?

"Wow!" said the little girl. "Look, mummy, she's as good as new!"

"I know sugar," said the girl's mother. "And I bet it didn't hurt a bit, did it?"

"No," pronounced June, "they were both very brave. And I am sure Lilly here didn't feel a thing."

She smiled benignly down at the little girl, her mouth gaping wide to reveal row upon row of rotten, filling-scarred teeth. The little girl smiled back, and June felt something fluttering in her chest.

This was why she loved her job. This was why she loved her *life*. This was why she lived, for moments like this.

"Thank you so much," said the little girl's mother. "What do we owe you?"

"Pah," exclaimed June, brushing the offer away with her hand. She saw the mother's eyes flicker to the hand for a moment…but even if the younger woman hadn't looked, she still would have known what she was feeling.

Disgust. Fear. Pity.

The other hand looked normal, of course, but June was used to using her left one because she could still control the fingers properly. *Those* fingers she could control *very* well. She covered up her embarrassment by carrying on quickly.

"I sold you the doll," she said. "It was right that I should fix it. It wasn't her fault the cat decided to get curious and see what dolls are made of."

The little girl giggled, and June waved them both off as they left the workshop.

She heard the bell above the shop door tinkle as it closed after them, and she relaxed back in her chair.

That was it, the end of another long day. The little girl with the damaged doll had been her last customer, but even though Christmas was still some weeks away, it had been busy. It was always busy in her little shop. After all, if it wasn't Christmas, someone always had a birthday coming up, or a new niece or nephew to spoil. Business was always good.

But that was only natural. She was the best, it was as simple as that.

She was the best...and because of that, she was now bone tired. She was looking forward to getting home tonight. It wasn't a long journey, but June always dreaded it, because there was always someone who noticed the way she was walking, and had the nerve, had the damn *nerve* to look at her with pity in their eyes...And then all at once, she wasn't the magical old lady who made the wonderful toys, she wasn't the mysterious grown up who could heal the favourite doll as good as new. She was just June again, the sad, lonely, misshapen thing that people stared at and were horrified by and...and who pitied her...

It had been the same since she was a small child.

"Pay no notice!" her mother used to tell her, but it was hard. Especially for someone who had her...gifts. To her, it didn't even matter if the person tried to be nice, if they managed to hide their feelings—even their pity—to hide it well, to keep it from spreading to their face.

What does it matter what someone's face is telling you when you can read what they are feeling as easily as if it were written in front of you in a book?

Her mother didn't understand, but her grandmother had.

"That's because you are of the blood, just like me!" the old woman had told her. "It's strong in some of us, weaker in others. Don't listen to what they feel about you. Feelings are not like actions. You cannot help what you feel."

But she *had* cared what people felt for her, of course she had. And it had taken more than some old witch with watered down magic in her blood to make her stop listening to people, to stop worrying about what they thought of her...

Her reverie was interrupted by the sound of the bell above the shop door ringing again.

Damn it!

She had been getting ready to go home. Couldn't these people read the sign on the door? It clearly stated that the shop closed at five-thirty. That was twenty five minutes ago.

Well, she was certainly not seeing anyone else now. No, she would just give them a sorry smile, and explain that she would be late getting home as it was, and that they would have to come back tomorrow.

With a groan, she levered herself up out of her chair, and made her way out of the back room workshop. She opened the door to the main shop-floor, and tried to plaster a pained expression on to her face.

"I'm terribly sorry, but we are actually..." she began to say, and stopped short.

She hadn't seen the man in the sharp suit and sunglasses for nearly forty years, but he didn't look a day older than when they had last met.

The smile shrivelled up on her face like a small, dead animal.

She remembered his name, of course.

"Hello, Jason," she said.

"Why, hello June," replied Jason, giving her a big toothy grin. "I must say, the years have been kind to you. Why do you spend all your time locked away in that little room? Surely it would be better used out in the wide world, breaking a few hearts?"

June took a deep breath.

If her time had come, she wouldn't make a scene. She had known this would happen sooner or later. But, she supposed, you always thought you had more time, didn't you? It was difficult to imagine the world without you in it.

"Don't expect me to start pleading with you or anything," she told him curtly. "I expect you get quite enough of that. I expect that's one of the things you enjoy the most. I thought I had longer, but if it's time, it's time."

The man in the sharp suit sighed theatrically.

"My dear, alas, you are mistaken," he slumped his shoulders. "I do not kill people. I am merely in charge of…making them certain offers."

June looked at him suspiciously.

"You mean…" she began, but he cut her off.

"Yes, yes," he said breezily, "you can tell your lovers to postpone their grieving; I'm not here to collect what you owe me. At least, not yet."

June frowned.

"If you're not here for that, then why?" she asked sharply.

Jason looked at her with hurt.

"Look, the sexual tension here is killing me, too, but can't we at least be professional about it?"

"Why are you here?" June repeated. "And don't try and bluster at me as if you are all smoothness and sunshine. I'm of the blood, as well you know, and I can see you're in trouble just as well as I can see those pretty yellow eyes behind those dark glasses of yours, so spare me your crap." She pulled herself up—as much as she could, anyway—and for a third time asked him, "Why are you here?"

Jason looked impressed.

"A woman who gets straight to the point," he said. "I like it. I'm here because I need your services."

"Oh!" said June. "What's wrong? Do you have a toy that needs fixing?"

"Not exactly," said Jason. "I need the services that you *used* to supply."

June froze. She looked at him from between narrowed eyes.

"I don't do that anymore," she told him. "That was a long time ago. I make toys now. I fix them, too. I don't do what you want anymore. I'm sorry, I can't help you."

Her heart was pounding. It had been so long…She couldn't believe it, but even *she* had almost forgotten…It seemed like a different life.

"Oh?" asked Jason. "Can't? Or won't?"

"Does it matter?" retorted June. "Look around you, this is a toy shop, not a…not a…"

"Not a workshop?" asked Jason innocently. "You're right, *this* is a shop. *That*," he added, pointing towards the back room. "*That* is a workshop."

"You think I'm equipped here to…"

"Of course you are," interrupted Jason. "And if you're not… well, improvise."

June looked at him sideways.

"And if I don't?" she said.

Jason shrugged.

"You know, I was just visiting some colleagues of mine," he said, conversationally. "It's a funny thing, but a lot if them still go in for the idea that it's actually worth letting a soul rot and suffer for, oh, I don't know, a century or two after it is harvested. It's never really appealed to me, I have to say. Nevertheless, I'm always open to new experiences. I mean, that's what's written on my Facebook page, so who am I to blow against the wind?"

June managed to keep her lips from trembling, but it was an effort.

"How do I know you won't do that to me anyway?" she said at last. "How do I know two centuries isn't peanuts for you?"

Jason looked at her with mock outrage.

"You don't trust me?" he said. "How dare you?"

She stared at him. He rolled his eyes.

"Fine," he said. "Well, seeing as how you are *of the blood*, as you put it, and we have this rather old-fashioned contract, why don't we just make an amendment? You can't say fairer than that."

June nodded grudgingly.

"I'll get the paperwork," she told him. She kept him waiting in the shop, while she went back into her work room to fetch it—she had never liked the idea of keeping the damned bit of paper in her actual house, but somehow a safety deposit box or a Swiss bank seemed, well, undignified—and came back puffing for breath.

She held the yellowed piece of parchment in her good hand. She hadn't looked at it for many years, but hardly a night went by without her thinking about the horrible thing. More so as the years went by, as her chest pains got worse and her breathing got worse and her good hand seemed just as quick and magical as ever.

"Ah, yes, I remember this one well," said Jason, taking the parchment, and unfurling it with a practiced flick. He scanned down the document to the end, produced a pen from his pocket, and scribbled a few lines. Then he signed with a flourish.

"You've made me come over all nostalgic," he told her. "People say email's more practical, but to me nothing screams *it's all a joke* than a contract for your everlasting soul ending up in your spam box."

June ignored him and examined what he had written. Satisfied, she rolled the parchment up again, and put it into her pocket.

"Fine," she said. "Now tell me what it is you want doing, and we can get this over with."

Jason smiled, and reached into his own pocket. He pulled out a small wooden box, and handed it to her.

Giving him a puzzled frown, she laid the box down on the counter and made to open it.

"Be careful," Jason forestalled her. "What's in there is light as a feather but very, very dangerous."

June nodded. She had been expecting no less.

She opened the box.

One of her eyebrows rose, very slightly.

She closed the box.

"Is that what I think it is?" she asked softly.

"Yes," said Jason.

June sighed. Then a smile quirked on her face.

"What is it?" asked Jason, frowning slightly.

June shrugged.

"I know what this means," she told him. "I was just thinking that I'm used to other people feeling sorry for *me*."

"Don't worry about them," Jason told her, his voice sounding unusually flat. "The one who has this coming knows quite well what's in store for her. She knew the rules. You shouldn't feel sorry for her."

"I wasn't talking about the person you're going to use this on," she told him.

Jason snorted. He looked like he wanted to say something, but then he changed his mind.

"Whatever," he told her. "I need this on a blade, and I need it now. Tonight. Can you do that?"

June felt her whole body sag.

"Tonight?" she repeated. "I haven't made a blade for thirty years, and you want *this one* by *tonight*?"

Jason moved closer. Suddenly, she didn't need to have her grandmother's blood in her veins to see his yellow eyes behind his sunglasses. It was if they were burning right through the tinted glass.

"Yes, tonight," he told her, his voice clipped and hard. "What's the problem? You made the best blades for the best killers on this continent, you did it for ten years, and you did it with that hand I gave you. You can make this one last blade for me tonight. I know you can. And you know what I will do to you if you fail." He turned round and walked to the door. "I will be back at midnight," he added.

The bell above the door made a sad little ringing noise as Jason left.

June sagged.

A blade. She had to make a blade. And not just any blade…

Her eyes crept to where the black wooden box still sat, small and still and horrible on the counter. She shuddered.

She never thought she would have to make a blade again. She had thought the rest of her life would be fixing the wheels on toy trains and stitching doll's eyes back in place.

She had been wrong.

And yet…

And yet she could feel a glimmer of professional excitement, somewhere deep down inside.

This would be a challenge…but she could do it. She *thought* she could do it.

She made her way back into her workshop, and began to fish out the tools she had believed she would never have to use again.

Then why did I keep them? She asked herself.

Then she surprised herself by bursting into a smile.

Wasn't life funny?

An hour ago she was sowing a doll's eye back into place, thirty minutes ago she was about to die, now she was staying up half the night making a blade that even people of the blood thought was a myth.

Who knew what was around the corner?

As far as she was concerned, only one thing was certain.

She was going to make this last blade, and then get on with her life, one day at a time, however much of it she had left.

And while making the blade, she would be *very* careful not to touch the thing that was in the box with anything other than good, solid iron.

However light and innocent it looked.

《《——》》

Dawn was just breaking on the small town of Clifton, Colorado—population somewhat less than the 1769 advertised proudly on the town sign—but Ben was already up and dressed and ready to go.

"Do we need to take food?" he asked Nathalie, but she shook her head.

"No, that's going to be part of the training," she told him. "No food, no water. And I want you to check everyone else on the bus, too. That's your job. And if I find someone has something…well, that's your fault."

Ben frowned. That was going to be *his* job? That didn't sound right.

"Why is that…?" he started to ask.

"Because you're my right hand man," she told him. She smiled as she said it, and she ruffled his hair.

But there was something cold in her voice, too, and Ben knew she wasn't joking.

He was her right hand man? That was crazy! He was eleven, for Christ's sake, he wasn't some tough—

—but he was tough, wasn't he? He suddenly knew it with complete conviction. He was her chosen warrior, and what did it matter if his balls hadn't dropped yet and his voice was still a high-pitched squeak? He could feel waves of confidence rolling through him. It was like a summer breeze gently warming his face. It was as if he was suddenly ten feet tall…

Nathalie removed her hand from his head and gazed down at her little lieutenant.

It was funny that out of the whole town, he was the strongest. He had proven the best pupil. Well, so far at least…

But that was the purpose of this little exercise, wasn't it? To try and separate the wheat from the chaff. To try and see who really had the potential to help her.

They left the house and made their way down the high street and to the car park outside the church. It was a cold day, but the sun was shining brightly and there was hardly a cloud in the sky.

The bus was waiting for them, just as Ben had told her it would be. Not that she had doubted him, not really. And when she had examined his thoughts, it had been obvious that the boy had *thought* he had done his job well.

There was a small crowd waiting expectantly by the bus, too.

Nathalie had been more sure about that, of course. After all, she had directly influenced most of the attendees herself, and she was confident that none of them would be able to overcome her intervention. They were all only weakly sensitive, moderate at best. That limited their ultimate usefulness, of course, but it had the advantage that they were much more easy to control. They were much less likely to offer her any little surprises.

Nasty surprises of a kind like Laura had offered.

She frowned as she remembered the girl. Now she had not been weak. She had been a good student. Very quick to learn, very good potential power…almost as strong as this young boy promised to be.

Nathalie's smile returned. It was so much better to find a pupil when they were young. That was what she had decided.

Before they had built their walls very high. Before they thought to question what was best for them. And before they had learnt to shut away their natural talents, in response to a world that told them such things could not exist…

The crowd gathered around the bus expectantly were mostly children. A few were younger adults. There was no one over the age of twenty five.

Miss Marston wasn't there of course. That was a shame, because Nathalie thought the teacher had probably had quite a lot of potential, before Ben had burnt it out of her. He hadn't meant to, naturally, and it couldn't be helped—omelettes and eggs, after all—but still, it was a shame.

The corner of her mouth twitched as she remembered the unfocussed look on the young woman's face, the tattered feeling of her mind as Nathalie had stroked the edges of her thoughts.

It was sad. The poor girl had been happy, and productive, and good, in her own way…but the things Nathalie was fighting for were higher, the victories she would gain would push the darkness back forever. The ends justified the means.

Nathalie strode past the group of onlookers. As she approached the bus, she felt the mind of the driver and *pushed*…

His hand shot out, and the door clacked open. She walked

smoothly up the steps, but when Ben made to follow her she shook her head, just slightly.

The boy swallowed, and for a moment he faltered, but Nathalie had been expecting that, and anyway the link she shared with him was strong. She sent another wave of confidence surging into him, and his back straightened.

She heard the words he spoke to the crowd gathered around the bus, but she knew that was not what moved them, not really.

No, what moved them were the little eddies of thought that Ben sent shooting out.

Nathalie raised an eyebrow.

He was improving, there was no doubt about it.

She could feel that he had brought up a mass of individual connections, one for every person, almost at once. That was impressive, especially considering there were some people there that Ben had never influenced before. It was a more complex business establishing a fresh link with someone than it was to re-open an existing connection.

On the other hand, he was working with minds that she had touched herself before, minds that had been made receptive. The real test would come later, in the city…

Get onto the bus, he was telling them.

No food or water, he was telling them.

This isn't the battle, he was telling them. *But it is training for the battle.*

He was doing more than issuing commands, of course.

Nathalie had instructed him about that very early on.

No, humans were animals, after all, however well developed those few ounces of grey matter behind the brows were. The thoughts skittered over the surface, and most people thought that was what moved them…but feelings ran much deeper than thoughts. If you wanted to move someone, you looked to their *feelings*.

And she felt the feelings pulsing out of Ben.

Joy. Excitement. Fellowship.

Love.

THE FALL OF THE ANGEL NATHALIE

They loved Ben. They really could not help themselves.

They loved Ben, and Ben loved her.

She smiled again to herself.

Wasn't that so perfect?

With an army driven by love, she would conqueror the forces of darkness forever.

All she had to do first was train it.

She stood to one side, and watched with pride as her people made their way forward and boarded the bus.

No one spoke. All she could hear was the crunching of boots on gravel.

It sounded very much like marching.

«« —»»

Emma Brooks, twenty three, waitress, mother of one, and secret reader of low-class borderline pornographic novels in her spare time, did not know why she had stopped stock still in the middle of the sidewalk. She did not know where her lunch—lovingly prepared by her doting, if slightly overweight, husband—had gone. She did not know why she was feeling so happy, so wonderfully, overwhelmingly, stupidly *happy*. All she knew was that it was as if someone had flipped a switch in her head, and suddenly all the happy in the world had come tumbling out.

She knew that, and she knew she would not be going home tonight. Instead, she would be getting on a bus with her new friends. She couldn't quite remember why, but she was sure it would all come right in the end.

«« —»»

Richard Stoke, nineteen, unemployed, frequent cannabis smoker, was not quite sure why he was making his way to a trashcan and emptying out the last of what had been an unbelievably potent batch of California Chronic. Usually the very thought of being dry made him sweat, but now he didn't feel like sweating at all. No, instead he felt…at peace. It was is if someone had just told him that at the end of life was a rainbow, huge and sparkling and belonging to *everyone*. Not just told him—offered him incontrovertible proof. He felt as if someone had just explained the meaning of it all to him, and everything was OK after all.

He smiled beatifically as he made the way to the back of the bus and sat down with all his new friends. His special friends, and the special, beautiful woman with the dark hair and the black eyes. Together, he knew, they would change the world.

«« — »»

Tara Hagan, twelve, beloved daughter, brilliant at math, whose biggest secret was that she had once practiced kissing on the family boxer puppy, was completely in the dark as to why she was not currently walking to the particular fast food outlet that her mother had specified they meet at. She knew she should, she just felt… she felt so *angry* at her mother. She couldn't say why—she loved her family, they had always loved her, and supported her, and nothing had changed recently. It was just that…every time she thought of them, she felt like she wanted to *scream*. And the idea of going back to the house, and facing them, smiling at them…

It made her feel sick.

So instead, she had just walked onto this bus filled with complete strangers, and sat herself down between a thin boy and a strange looking woman with black eyes.

"Good," the woman said, completely ignoring her. "Sometimes love or friendship or attraction will not work."

The boy looked puzzled.

«« — »»

"But it feels…*wrong*, somehow," Ben complained, as their latest target sat down between him and Nathalie. "Making someone feel love, or…or making them happy, that feels OK. But making someone hate their parents…"

141

He trailed off. Nathalie tilted her head sympathetically.

"I understand how you feel, Ben," she told him. "How can any good come from hate? How can we heal this world by making rifts between people? I'm glad you feel this way. I'm proud of you for it. But listen, Ben," she leant closer. "There are some people who listen to love, just like there are some people who listen to reason. But not everyone will. I wish they would, but they won't. Believe me, if anyone knows that, I do."

She leant backwards and licked her lips. They looked very red to Ben.

"Do you think your father would have listened to love, Ben?" she asked him softly, and Ben felt something *lurch* inside of him, felt his thoughts—

—you didn't have to kill *him, you bitch! You didn't have to—*

—see-saw wildly from side to side, as if someone had shoved a live wire into his head and a million volts were jolting through him.

He shut his eyes so tight he saw livid flashes of color bursting in front of him.

"Of course he wouldn't have," she went on relentlessly. "You know that because you *tried*, Ben. You tried being reasonable with him. You tried, and he wouldn't listen. I want you to remember that."

Ben wished she would stop talking about his—

I loved him! I loved him even if he didn't give two shits about me! Whatever else he was he was my—

—father. Every word she spoke sent a jolt of pain spearing through his brain. But he had to listen to her. She was his…his what? His leader? His friend? His…*god*?

All of those. She was his…his *everything*. And he had to listen to her.

"I used to think that anyone could be changed by being reasonable," she went on. "I used to think that love and kindness and patience could change the world on their own. That all you had to do was explain things to people, to listen to them and support them, and then given them the chance to make the right choice. But I was wrong, and I learnt that the hard way."

She paused for a moment. She looked distant. Ben thought she even seemed…well, *sad.*

Then, "Remember your father," Nathalie commanded, and Ben could not help himself. He felt his mind peeling open, felt the scarred portions where Nathalie had done…*something*…to him

—she's hurting you! She's tearing you apart, breaking and burning and repackaging you, making you different, making you into something she *wants, just like you're doing to these people! She's—*

And suddenly his mind was full of images of his father, all the images and thoughts he had built up over the nearly-twelve years of his short life. They were not easy to pull up—Nathalie had filled the paths that led there with barbs and false turns and broken glass—and it hurt like hell.

But he did not have a choice.

After all, that was what she was telling him to do.

The images hung there, so close to the surface of his thoughts that he could practically touch them, hanging there in there air in front of him.

"Now," commanded Nathalie, "look at them. Look closely."

Ben looked.

Most of those memories and images, he realized, were ugly.

He wasn't feeling sorry for himself. He had always known his father was not much of a man, not really.

He examined the images more closely. *There* was the time at his sixth birthday when his father had yelled at his mother in front of all his friends and their parents. After that, he hadn't had many friends for a while.

And here was the time his father had used his belt to teach him not to…

And here was the smell of stale beer as his father laughed at his paintings and told him…

And here was his father's hand as it fell towards his mother's face, her head already falling backwards from the blow, and she…

143

And here was…

Oh, *here* was the smile on his father's lips as Ben sat between them as a young boy—*very* young—and tore open his presents on Christmas morning. How long ago was that? Had he been four? Five? He wasn't sure. But his father was smiling. His arms felt warm and safe and good as they went around Ben's shoulders and held him tight.

Ben's mouth twitched into a smile…and he felt the weight of Nathalie's mind bearing down on him, flattening the memory like a butterfly pinned in a collector's book, glaring at it in the relentless white light of her thoughts. Ben gasped. It wasn't painful, as such, just…jarring. And he couldn't do a thing to stop it.

Then she was rifling through other areas of his mind, flicking through his memories. She extracted something, some image or scene—he could not say which for sure, it was all happening so quickly. Nathalie was very skilful.

There was a moment of stillness, and then a sensation of *burning*, and then…

The image of his father changed.

Where he had been smiling, now he was sneering.

He was laying in the bed next to Ben's mother, and screaming at the five-year old Ben that he was right, wasn't he? Ben didn't really have any balls, he didn't dare fight him. The smell of alcohol and cheap cigarettes washed towards him from the memory, so clear it felt like he was right there, squashed in the bed between his monster of a father and the small, cowering warmth of his mother.

Then his father leaned back and picked up a bottle of beer—

—*that wasn't right, he never drank when I was a little kid, and he* never *drank in bed, and I think something is wrong and I*—

—and hit his mother in the face.

Ben reeled, but even as he did so he felt Nathalie had already moved on, to another memory, and another, and another.

He felt them drop inside of him, like a trail of dominos falling one after another.

Snap. Snap. Snap. Snapsnap. Snapsnapsnap…

He could feel the hate inside him rising. It was like a wall of fire ready to eat up the entire world.

It rose, it rose, it rose…

And then with a crash, it swelled to a crescendo—

—it's not real it's not real she's changing things my father was a bastard but there was some good in him and now she's taking it from me she's taking it from me forever and—

—and died away to nothing.

Breathe in. Breathe out.

His mind felt silent and calm and…

And Nathalie was right.

"You see," Nathalie said to him softly, "your father was not a man who would listen to reason. He would not listen to reason, or to love. So I had to use my other toolbox. Every engineer should have more than one toolbox, Ben. You are an engineer, just like I am. And this," she added, pointing to the girl siting between them, who had not moved an inch since she had sat down, "this young lady has just been your first lesson in how to use that other toolbox."

Nathalie tilted her head and shrugged.

"The world is full of people who we will not be able to motivate with love or joy or peace," she told Ben. "People like your father. For those people, you need to develop your other toolbox."

Ben nodded mutely. Nathalie was right. His father had been a bastard. He had never listened, and he never would have listened. And if the people they were fighting were like him…

He licked his lips.

"Can I try again?" he asked.

"Of course," Nathalie's voice was soft. "Before we leave, we need to make sure this bus is filled with people who have the potential to be our soldiers."

"Soldiers?" asked Ben. That seemed…scary.

He had known they were going to be fighting, but did that make them soldiers? He frowned. He supposed it did.

Nathalie nodded, and her black eyes flicked over the figures streaming past outside.

"There's a war coming, Ben," she told him. "And I have the feeling that it won't be long before someone brings it to us."

For a moment, her eyes clouded, as if she were imagining… what? Ben wondered. She looked worried, but Ben could not imagine anything in the world that she could be afraid of. She was so…so still, so certain, so…*powerful*.

Then her eyes flicked back to Ben and she smiled.

"Now," she said briskly, "why don't you try seeing if you can bring someone to us using…oh, let's try fear, shall we?"

Ben smiled back.

Fear it was.

«‹—›»

This room was shining white, and very empty.

The walls were plastered, stark and bright, and there was essentially no furniture. A single bright neon strip light was suspended overhead. It had not been turned off since 1968, even though the person who owned the room visited only very rarely.

Money wasn't a problem, and the electricity bills always got paid on time.

Every few years, a burglar made an unlucky choice, and decided to try and break in.

They were never hurt physically, but it often took them several months to recover from the things they had seen when they entered that plain, white room.

Not that any of those things were real, of course.

To summon real creatures of the type those burglars saw would be to open a box that could not be easily closed, and Jason had no urge to commit an act that would be seen as an Intervention and punished accordingly.

To do someone physical harm or break into the thoughts of a potential client and meddle with them strongly was an unforgivable Intervention, of course. But to protect one's home from prying eyes…

That could be justified.

Jason breathed in deeply as he walked through the plain wooden door. Home sweet home.

Not that he had a home, not really. It wasn't like he needed to sleep or eat or rest; if truth be told, he was actually something of a workaholic.

But even if he was not in the habit of torturing souls he had won, that did not mean that he wasn't a prudent creature.

You never knew, did you, quite when a sip more vitality would be most useful?

It was always worth having something in reserve.

That's what this room was for: not a place to sleep or to relax after a long day of tempting and scheming and meddling. No, this was a repository.

There was not much furniture in the room.

But there was *one* thing. It was a small, neat cube, about two feet to a side. It stood in one corner of the room. It was white, too.

Jason walked over to his white cube, and opened a latch that any intruder—if they had managed to get this far, of course—would have found almost impossible to locate.

The door swung open, and more pure white light spilled out from inside.

A little cold mist seeped forward and began tumbling softly to the floor.

Jason inspected his collection.

The souls were laid there in front of him in row upon row of neat little tubes. At least, they *looked* like tubes. Actually, they protruded into several other dimensions not normally perceivable in the human world, and what they tethered there was…

Was what Jason had come to find. To find…and to consume.

His fingers drifted lightly over the tubes, touching, tasting, choosing…

His collection represented the fruit of countless years of hard work. There were souls here that had been harvested before the discovery of penicillin, there were souls here that had sat in this cool, white room for over a century, dreaming, unaware of the passage of time…

Jason needed strength now. It had been some time since he had last drunk in the vitality his kind needed to exist, and he had rather a nasty job to do.

He needed to be at his best, chock full of vitality, overflowing…

It was an extensive collection. Jason was judicious with his meals, and never liked to consume more than he needed. He flicked through his tubes idly. He remembered all his clients very clearly. They all tasted slightly different, they all offered subtly varying shades of hate, of anguish, of fear…

He stopped.

He licked his lips.

Now *this* one…

This was no ordinary human fragment of soul.

This was the prize of his collection. He had tasted it, of course he had.

But he had not been able to bring himself to drink it all. It was too rich, it would have made him sick to take it all at once.

He lifted the little vile gently and brushed it against his lips.

It tasted as fresh as the day it was taken.

When she had fallen, when he had tempted her into making the mistake that had lost her her wings, Jason had won part of her higher soul, won it as a prize, won it in the same way he won a tithe of any soul he brought to the edge and gently persuaded to jump.

Jason held Nathalie's soul in his hands. What was left of it, anyway…He wondered if now was the time to consume the remainder? The thought of it made him feel elated and nauseous all at once.

It was very potent.

If he drank all of it, it would fill him right up, right to the brim. He would not have to have any other meal, not for a long time. Additionally, he would be able to sense her with much greater clarity than he currently could. Not that this would really be necessary. After all, he could still find her, and without much difficulty. Even now, several months after they had last met, and more than a year since she had fallen and Jason had drunk in part of her soul, even now he could sense where she was. He could even feel a dim echo of what she was feeling. But if he drank this last ounce of her, that awareness would flare brightly up in him. He might even be able to catch glimpses of the things she saw, feel echoes of the emotions she was feeling...

He looked carefully at the little tube. It glimmered at him. He touched it to his lips once more, and closed his eyes. He breathed in.

It tasted so sweet. He could picture her so clearly. He remembered her in a thousand ways, a million scenes. They had worked together for a long time, after all. They had been friends. More than that, they had been...

What had they been?

He found he could not say.

He opened his eyes, and lowered his hand.

No.

He would not use up the last of her. Not now.

It wasn't that he still felt...anything for her, of course.

He wasn't being sentimental. Not at all.

No, he was just being sensible. Prudent. That was it.

After all, this was the most potent morsel in his collection, by a clear mile.

He should save this for when he needed it the most.

He laid the vial containing what was left of Nathalie's higher soul down on the floor, very gently.

Then he frowned to himself. Why was he wasting time? After all, it was nearly midnight. He had a blade to collect.

His hands flashed out and chose more vials, picking them randomly.

These would do. What did it matter which ones?

Efficiently, he snapped one of the vials open. Immediately, the unique scent of the frozen soul began to seep out, accompanied by a low, dour moan. It was intoxicating, and Jason greedily tipped the vial up and emptied it into himself.

It tasted delicious.

He quickly repeated the process with three other vials, then forced himself to stop.

That was enough.

He felt as if his whole body was on fire.

He was pulsing with energy. It coursed through him, making every sense sharper, every thought flash quicker through his mind.

He took some deep breaths to steady himself.

He retrieved the unopened vial from the floor—the special vial, *her* vial—and made to put it back in the white container with the rest of his collection.

Then he hesitated.

No. If the coming battle was to be a hard one, he realized, he might need some more rejuvenation before he was done. He could hardly go into battle with his whole collection stuffed in his pockets, could he?

But one little vial…One very potent little vial…

He made his decision.

He shut the door of the white container, and closed the latch very tight with a small act of pure will. It was now to all intents and purposes shut beyond the skill of any human intruder to unlock.

He put Nathalie's vial in an inside pocket and closed the door behind him when he left.

It was five minutes to midnight. It was time to collect his blade.

«««——»»»

The old bell above the door rang softly as the door opened, and Jason walked in.

It was precisely midnight, and June was expecting him.

She had made her deadline, but only just. Inside her workshop, some of the tools she had used were still warm. A few had even shattered or melted during the process of making the blade, but that was only natural. After all, it was a very, very special blade.

Jason smiled brightly, and June shuddered. There was something different about him, she thought. He looked…fuller, somehow, more real. His skin glowed. If she didn't know what he *really* was, she would have thought he looked quite handsome.

He opened his mouth to speak, but June got there first.

"It's done," she told him quickly. "I don't have time for any of your little games. Just take what you came for, and go."

Jason looked sad.

"Why are you always so mean to me?" he complained. "Just because I steal and eat sinful souls, does that mean I don't have feelings? Shame on you!"

June snorted.

"Why should I feel shame when you don't even know what it means?" she asked him archly. "Now do you want what you came for or not?"

"I want it," said Jason evenly. "I just thought we might exchange pleasantries first. But never mind. I see I am dealing with a philistine."

You could stab him with it, June thought wildly. *Maybe if you did that…*

But no. The weapon she had forged was surpassing strong, and it could kill…well, anything, probably. That was why this daemon had been issued…the thing that he had brought her. Because somewhere, she knew, a daemon had gone rogue, and needed bringing down.

She was of the blood, and she knew something of the way of things. She knew a little of daemons. And she knew enough to know that if she tried to turn the blade on Jason, she would not survive the night.

A daemon was not allowed to touch a human with much more than his tongue, certainly not allowed to physically hurt them… unless they were threatened, of course.

Then they could do what they wanted.

She had no illusions about her own abilities as a warrior. Even if she did wield the blade she had made for him…

"Wait here," was all she told him.

151

She went into her workshop, and came back carrying a box.

It was larger than the one he had brought her, naturally, and she had not been able to find anything as stark black as that one, either.

This box was perhaps a little over a foot long and made of old, dark wood. It was plain but beautiful, in its own way.

She licked her lips. The thought of putting a weapon like this back in the hands of a daemon…

But then, she had no choice.

She held out her hands, and Jason took the box.

He examined it for a moment, turning it until it faced him.

His fingers found the little golden catch, and flicked it upwards.

He opened the box.

"Oh, my," he said, and there was only a trace of sarcasm in his voice. "My dear, you have outdone yourself."

Slowly, he reached inside the box and grasped the handle.

The dagger he pulled out had a plain grip made of metal and wood. There was a single stone, blood-red, embedded in the hilt.

The blade was only about eight inches long. It was curved in a cruel arc.

And it was made of pure darkness. It was made of shadows.

Jason lifted the weapon and held it up to the light.

It seemed to draw illumination in. The room actually seemed darker.

"This is fine workmanship," Jason told her. "How did you…?"

She knew she shouldn't tell him anything more than she had too, but June was an artist, after all. And she was proud of what she had done. It had been over thirty years since she had made a weapon…and the one she had made this night, at the eleventh hour, after sowing dolls eyes and fixing toy wheels for the last three decades…Well, it was her masterpiece.

"The hilt is from an old weapon from the crusades I acquired some years ago," she told him. "It is old, but very strong. And unique, too. There is some magic in it that I was never able to replicate. I thought it was…right…to use in this case."

Jason nodded, and signalled for her to go on.

"The hard part was finding the right substrate to hold what you brought me in place," she continued. "I tried a wooden wedge, industrial glue, even molten metals. The wood and the glue burnt, the metal would not set. It got hotter, in fact."

"What did you do in the end?" Jason asked.

"In the end," said June, allowing herself a thin smile, "I did what I always knew I had to do. I knew from the moment you showed me what was in the box."

She held up her hand, her right hand, the useless one.

Her little finger ended in a bandaged stump at the first joint.

"Human bone," she told him. "The quill burnt a hole through the middle, and lodged there. I was then able to lock the ring of bone within the metal head of the dagger."

"Interesting," Jason nodded, looking more closely at the hilt, but obviously taking great pains to avoid the blade.

"Yes, interesting," echoed June, flexing her mutilated hand.

She paused. She wanted him to go, wanted to scream at him to get out, that their deal was over, that they were not friends nor would they ever be.

But she was interested despite herself.

"Tell me," she said haltingly, "where did you...how did you...?"

"How did we get the feather?" Jason asked her, sounding amused. His eyes went again to the horrible darkness of the blade. When he looked closely, he *could* make out the shadowed feather there, reaching up in its cruel arc, the soft blackness of the material blurring seamlessly into the deadly blade.

June nodded mutely.

"Simple," he said, not looking at her. "The higher authorities commanded it. They commanded their little shadowed pet to come down and pay us a visit—I say *us*, but that was a long time before I was even born—to visit the darkness, and offer up this portion of herself.

"One feather of the Hecatomb. One feather of the Angel of Shadows. That was the gift the light gave to the darkness, many thousands of years ago. So that we might punish our transgressors just as the light punishes theirs. They do not like to Intervene, you see. They do not like to get their hands dirty. Even if we have a rogue that is going to end a thousand human lives, they still will not Intervene. Never."

June frowned. Was she imagining it, or did Jason sound... angry? That was not possible, surely? Why should a daemon care if a thousand humans died? Surely that was playing into the hands of the darkness?

Then Jason laughed, a short, nasty laugh, and he looked at her. There was the smallest quirk of a smile on his face.

"I've met her myself, of course," he said. "The Angel of Shadows, I mean. Charming lady. Very sharp hands, as I remember."

Jason looked at her for a moment, then dropped his eyes.

He put the blade carefully back in the box, shut the lid, and placed the box in one of his deep pockets.

"Anyway, I must dash," he told her briskly. "You know how it is, people to tempt, souls to harvest."

June raised an eyebrow.

"And friends to kill?" she asked him.

Jason froze for a moment, in the act of turning to go.

"Yes," he said. "Yes, that too."

He walked to the door and opened it.

"I will need you to remove the feather again once my task his done," he told her.

She nodded. She had suspected as much. Such a powerful weapon would not be allowed to stay as a weapon between uses. The higher authorities would have been very clear about that.

"I will be waiting for you," she told him.

The door closed, and the bell rang, and June was alone.

«««——»»»

Jason surveyed the earth as it tilted lazily on its axis.

It was so quiet up here, so beautifully, totally silent.

After all, there was essentially no air this high up. How could there be noise when there was no air?

Even though he was falling, accelerating at a rate unimpeded, yet, by much air resistance, he was so high up that the swelling of the planet as he fell closer was almost imperceptible.

Europe was covered in darkness, millions of motes of light shining out from the countless cities. To the East, the golden wave of morning was advancing across Asia, shining happy and free and full of promise.

But Jason was not looking to the East. His eyes were fixed on the darkness. Many, many, miles far away across the vast ocean, he could feel her. Her mind pulsed like a beacon. He could sense her even across the curvature of the planet.

Can she sense me? he wondered.

She shouldn't be able to. After all, he was the one who had defeated her, and not the other way round.

And yet…

And yet she had always managed to surprise him, hadn't she?

The sound of air rushing past began to sound in his ear. It was soft at first, a gentle whispering, but it was quickly growing louder. He began to feel his skin heat up as the friction warmed him. If he let himself fall much further he would run the risk of his clothes combusting.

He concentrated for a moment, and darkness seethed around him. An instant later, the sound was gone again. He had thrown himself higher again, and he was clear of the atmosphere once more. There was a distance limit to how far he could dissipate, of course, but at the moment he was chock-full of power, and he was easily able to throw himself several kilometres at a single jump.

But he had not thrown himself any further across the dark ocean. Not yet. Something still held him back…

Renegades were always dangerous. They made every daemon shudder, not just because they had lost that fine sliver of self-control that prevented them from unleashing all their pent up powers in suicidally brutal attacks. Not just because that power was often exponentially greater than other daemons, because they tended to feed on souls they had dispatched themselves, a much more potent—though, of course—poisoned source of energy than a soul harvested at the end of a natural life by subtle acts of temptation.

No, the real reason that daemons were terrified of renegades, terrified deep down in the darkness of their own souls, was that they were walking reminders of how easy it would be to become one yourself.

Daemons spent their days tempting humans…and the irony was, they were the ones who really had to fight temptation, fight it every moment of every day.

How easy it would have been, for example, to shoot out a hand and crush that silly toymaker's skull. He could have done it in the flash of an eye. He could probably have moved so fast that she wouldn't have felt a thing.

And then…

The sweet release of soul that would have come pouring out. It would have dripped out of her skull with the blood, like honey.

He would have drunk it up like nectar, and it would have strengthened him immeasurably.

And set him on the path to madness, of course.

Jason sighed, something that's quite hard to do when there's no air about.

Oh well.

Better not to keep the lady waiting.

He dissipated again. This time, as well as flinging himself upwards, he pushed himself out further across the Atlantic.

He reappeared, took a few moments to bunch himself up, and did it again. And again.

Snap. Snap. Snap.

Jason followed Nathalie across the night and further into the darkness.

He was coming for her.

《《—》》

Her town was sleeping. No one stirred, not a muscle.

She could feel the wind drifting through the empty streets, softly, like a breath.

She was perched on the roof of the church, legs wrapped around the steeple. She had a cigarette in one hand.

She took a breath to centre herself, then reached out with her mind.

She could feel them there. Her people. Her soldiers. She could feel every one.

It was incredible, what she had done. How much she had achieved as soon as she had stopped playing by their stupid rules.

Not that this town had been a den of sin, as it were, not exactly.

But where there were humans, there was sin. Where there were humans, there was suffering.

Except for here.

Here, no one hurt one another. No one suffered.

She had made sure of that. That was the way this town worked.

There had been sacrifices along the way, of course. How could there not be? But they had been necessary. That was the whole point of a sacrifice. You got more out than you put in.

The most important thing, she realized, was that there were people who were beyond saving.

People who would never listen, who would only end up getting in the way.

But they were like cells in any organism. Once they outgrew their usefulness, they died away. And if they refused to die when it was their time, if they obstinately stayed alive, despite what was best for the organism as a whole…well, there was a word for that, wasn't there?

Cancer.

And yes, of course, with each death she felt another bittersweet thrill gushing through her body. That wasn't why she did it, it was just a by-product. Naturally, it was useful. It would have been a waste to let all that energy just seep away into the cosmos, when instead she could drink it up like a dry sponge. She closed her eyes as she remembered the sensation. She shuddered. It was so sweet, like a firework going off in your soul, like a ripe fruit bursting on your tongue…

She blew out a last puff of smoke and sent her cigarette spinning down to the dark ground below. She watched the embers for a moment, glowing forlornly in the darkness.

That's what this town is, she told herself. *One glowing ember in a vast sea of darkness.*

But not for long.

It was amazing what you could achieve when you stopped fighting with your hands tied behind your back.

Take today.

This morning she had set out with a boy who had developed reasonable power, and maybe ten others who had flickers of potential. The rest of the crew on the bus had been essentially useless, and she had known it, really. But then, when your highest cards are threes and fours, you play with them until you can get a better hand.

Which is what she had done.

The city was full of people. So many people, so much weakness, so much hate…

And so much potential.

She had to admit, even she had been a little surprised at the results herself.

She had returned this evening with a bus that was full to capacity. And she had not had to snare a single one herself. Her soldiers had done it for her.

They were getting better. Especially the boy. He was even managing to maintain multiple threads of influence at once, a trick which was very difficult. And what did it matter if he had needed a little extra…encouragement? Everyone needs motivation. If a daemon could whisper in an ear, why couldn't she run the threads of a mind through her fingers, and snap one when that was what the occasion demanded? What was the difference, really?

158

Her soldiers had found so many people with the makings of power in them that she had decided to leave the very weakest of her people in the city, to make way for the new recruits on the bus home. Of course, she could have easily snared another bus— or ten, for that matter—but that would be a strategic mistake.

She had all she could work with, for now. She did not want to stretch herself too thin, not until she could consolidate everything.

No, for now her little empire was just like the ember glowing below her. A single beacon of light in a sea of darkness.

Not for long though. Soon it would be a fire that would engulf the world.

Soon, the work of the daemons would be halted forever. The work of the angels, too, for that matter.

Who could say? Maybe they would even give her her wings back…

She laughed at that.

Yes, that's what they would do.

They would cover her in glory, and give her back her beautiful ruby wings. Not that she missed them much, not anymore.

There were much sweeter things than wings, she had realized.

She frowned. She felt someone stirring, an old lady far out on the border of her town, someone she had not paid much notice before now.

Her tongue darted out, dark in the night, and her mouth was suddenly full of saliva.

She wondered what that old lady had done in her long life? Well, long by human standards, anyway…

It suddenly occurred to her that someone who had lived so long had probably done *something* that was not altogether pardonable. Maybe she had drowned a kitten, maybe she had deliberately aborted a pregnancy she did not want…

Of course, she wouldn't know for sure unless she paid her a visit.

She slipped off the church and landed softly on the grass.

159

Maybe she was entirely innocent.

But if she wasn't...

Nathalie licked her lips again, and started moving towards where the old woman turned fitfully in her sleep.

Like fireworks in the mind, she thought. *Like a ripe fruit bursting on your tongue.*

«««—»»»

The sea skimmed by below him, crashing and unsettled, as if it was disturbed by his passage.

Jason had lost his altitude now, and had slowed himself down enough that the atmosphere wasn't setting his clothes on fire as he fell. This had not been an altogether pleasant experience, as it involved a series of rapid dispersions straight down, each time spending as little time as possible shooting through the ever-thickening air, and ending with another staccato burst of materialisations alternating between sky and deep sea. It was horribly painful, of course, but daemons were to most intents and purposes immortal—especially when they were brim-full of power—and having wet clothes was better than having no clothes.

In any case, he quickly dried out as he shot through the air.

Now he was approaching the East coast of America, and he had reduced the distance of the jumps he was making to a little over a kilometre at a time. Occasionally he threw in a few hundred metres of altitude to keep from actually hitting the waves.

The transatlantic crossing had taken a little over twenty-five minutes. He thought he could have done it in around eighteen at a push. He had not encountered anyone on his journey, except for one point when he had flashed closer than he had meant to a small tugboat bobbing helplessly in the rough weather. He had even caught a glimpse of a wide-eyed sailor who happened to be looking straight at him as he flew by overhead in between dissipations. He had given the man a little wave, and promptly vanished.

The sea grew whiter as he approached the coast, and suddenly he was shooting over a beach, the clear sand pale in the starlight. Then that was gone, too, and he was flying out over fields and dark woodland. He felt the fright of small creatures as they sensed him stir the air above their heads.

Snap.

He was a kilometre up again. It was easy to shape his body into a natural spike, using the wind-flow around his contours to enhance his Westward motion. He judged that he was probably flying over New Jersey, though he had no more than a vague grasp of the geography of the North American continent. He had only spent around seventy or eighty years of his long life in the New World, and he had never found it all that appealing. But he was not basing his destination on maps or state lines.

He was simply following a light, a warmth…a certain *feeling*, something that drew him onwards, onwards, onwards.

The ground screamed by below.

Soon. It would be soon.

She broke the lock of the window without even thinking about it, and glided up the stairs soundlessly. She felt the old lady turn uneasily in the bed above her, and sprayed a calming mist of thought through the ether. She felt it settle like a net around the woman.

Good. She did not want anyone to suffer.

Not that she was going to do anything to her. Not necessarily. It all depended.

Nathalie reached the top of the stairs and crept across the landing. The door to the bedroom was open, and beyond, in the moonlight, she could see the old woman's chest rise and fall slowly.

She looked very peaceful.

Nathalie approached and carefully sat down beside her. She gently ran a hand down her wrinkled cheek. The old lady looked very frail. The cover had half fallen away, revealing the curve of a pot belly. It looked pale and sickly in the moonlight.

All around her, through the walls of the house, past the trees and the little roads, she could feel the sleeping heartbeat of the whole town. She was touching the boy and a few of her most powerful servants directly, and through them the network of awareness spread out like a spider's web until it included the whole sleeping town.

It was beautiful, but it was noisy. Too noisy for the task at hand. Also, she realized with a stab of guilt, she did not want any flashback from what she was about to do. She did not want to leave a trail.

Not that she was doing anything wrong.

Of course she wasn't.

It was just that she didn't want to disturb anyone's sleep. They needed their rest. They needed to be at their best. She had told the boy that a war was coming, and she was sure of that, though she did not think it would be any time soon. And yet…it was always best to be prepared, wasn't it?

Tomorrow, she decided, she would take Ben and another four of her best, her most able soldiers. She would teach them how to listen, how to be warned of any threat.

There was a shuffling noise from the bed as the old woman shifted in her sleep.

Nathalie's eyes, which had been full of thought, darted back to her, and glazed over.

She touched the woman's cheek again, then let it fall further down, tracing the line of her jaw, then coming to rest over her neck.

The flesh there was so soft, she thought. All it would take would be a little pressure…

Her tongue darted out again. Her lips were very dry, but her mouth was very wet.

Time to see what this old lady had in her soul. Nathalie was sure she could find something unsavoury. The woman was looking more and more like a…well, like a sinner. She was sure of it.

Nathalie gathered up the tendrils of thought that connected her to her lieutenants, and sheared them all off.

The bustling, busy sensation died down. Now the world consisted of this one room. All that mattered was her, and the woman who slept softly on the bed.

She fashioned another tendril of thought, hesitated a moment, then slammed it into the old woman's mind. It would probably hurt her, and it might even cause some damage, but that didn't really matter.

After all, what was the point of being subtle?

The woman would probably be dead in less than a second.

And then…then she would feed.

«《——》»

Jason felt the beacon blooming ahead of him. He was very close now. He was sure Nathalie was no further off than ten or twenty kilometres.

The question was, did she know he was coming?

He quested desperately towards her. At times in the past, he had sometimes been able to gather up a faint echo of what she was feeling. It had given him a small but distinct advantage. But since she had gone rogue and disappeared, that faint trickle of emotion had completely vanished. He had assumed it was something to do with the distances involved, but now he was less certain.

She had grown. He was sure of it. She had killed, and she had drunk, and she was not the same as the last time they had fought.

And that time, even, she had given him a run for his money.

But I have the blade, he told himself.

For some reason, this did not make his heart lighter.

I am here to kill her, he thought blankly.

He could do it. Of course he could.

But then, he had never killed before. Not ever. Not once.

He realized he was falling almost straight down, and shook himself. Now was not the time for doubts.

163

He scowled into the darkness, tilted his body, and made a further few jumps up and forward.

Snap, snap, snap.

The landscape jolted beneath him as he dissipated.

And then he was there.

He was almost directly above her. Her presence shone out like a lighthouse.

He thought he could even make out the house she was in, right now, right there beneath his body.

He glanced around. He was in a small nowhere town. Streetlights marked out the geography of the little settlement. He doubted that more than two or three thousand people made their home here.

But what was *she* doing here?

He strained towards her once more…and then he *could* feel something. It was stronger than he had anticipated. Her feelings were pulsing out at him like a beating heart. She was not trying to shield herself. She probably hadn't even considered doing so.

Anticipation. Anticipation, and just a shade of guilt. And riding over it all, strong and unstoppable…hunger. She was hungry.

What did that mean?

It didn't matter.

Just get it over with.

Jason pulled his arms back and fell straight downwards.

«««—»»»

Nathalie's thoughts slammed into the old lady. Her mind shrieked in alarm before submitting almost instantly. How could it do otherwise? Nathalie was completely overwhelming. She had used so much force, it was like using a school bus to swat a house fly.

The old woman's mind stood naked and quivering before her.

Nathalie bent her will inwards, and suddenly every thought and memory was being torn up and laid bare. It was like looking at an exploding sun, only instead of tendrils of hot plasma shrieking outwards, images and smells and emotions flew past.

Nathalie was engulfed by them. They surrounded her, and she flew inwards, deeper, deeper, deeper…

Moving faster than even she had thought possible, she began sorting through them

Under her cold hand and a million miles away, she felt the old woman's body spasm. She was in pain. She was terrified.

Nathalie didn't care. Her hunger was so powerful, her need was so sharp.

There had to be something here, some incriminating scene, some guilty memory…

She dug deeper.

The old woman gasped and squirmed as her consciousness filled up in an instant with things that had not happened for decades, things that had been consigned to the oldest barracks of memory, and over the years had settled softly in a fine sediment, musky and mouldy and forgotten.

Nathalie's hand twitched.

What was this?

A little sister. A flame of jealousy. *How dare you take my parent's love? How* dare *you?*

A trip to the lake, in high summer, when it was so hot the whole world seemed to be wilting, and the sky was vast and blue forever. A rock she picked from the shore, and the heavy smoothness of it in her hand. The way the light caught it as it glinted through the air. The sound it made as it hit her sister on the head, and the wrong appearance of her skull afterwards, like a rotten barn that has caved in on itself. The complete silence. The way the water moved as she had fallen in and slipped downwards. The dancing of the grass in the wind as she turned and walked away. The shouts of their parents, the search…the funeral.

It all came tumbling out, like the insides of a gutted fish, stinking and awful and raw.

Nathalie smiled.

Her hand tensed. She had her reason. The old woman's neck felt so soft…

She hesitated.

The Fall of the Angel Nathalie

She was aware of the faintest whistling sound.
It doesn't matter, was all she had time to think.
Then the world exploded.

The house swelled below him, bigger and bigger until he was almost on top of it. At the last possible moment, Jason dissipated and reappeared a few feet lower down, in the upstairs bedroom. He could have smashed through the roof itself, of course, but it was just possible the impact would have thrown him off-course so that he missed her. It was a skilful move to pull off at such a high speed. He would have been proud of himself if he had had the time.

He had one frozen impression of Nathalie before he slammed into her, standing beside a bed and leaning over someone. She was not looking at him.

And then the awful momentum he had built up over his fall—which had begun on the other side of the Atlantic—carried him downwards.

His body hit her, and an instant later they were crashing through the floor, wooden boards exploding around them as they plummeted downwards. He caught a fleeting glimpse of a kitchen, and then they hit the stone slabs of the ground floor.

There was an awful bone-deep *crush*, and then they were roaring through the stone slabs, too, and the foundations of the house shook as they burrowed deeper into the earth below.

And then it was over.

Jason's body screamed pain. He was alive, of course—after all, he was basically immortal, and so was his quarry. And it was not as if anything could break, either. His bones were harder and more solid than diamonds. But that did not mean that he could not feel pain.

He gasped a breath as the dust began to settle. He felt something shift beneath him.

It was Nathalie.

He was resting on her, her body crumpled and awkward beneath him. Her eyes were closed.

He had done it.

He had caught her off guard.

This was his moment.

He fumbled a hand into his jacket. It was wrinkled and torn, but amazingly, it was still essentially whole.

He retrieved the wooden box June had given him. The catch snapped open, and Jason was holding the dagger.

Its black blade danced in front of his eyes. It was so dark.

Of course it was. It was the essence of shadow.

He slowly turned the blade and lowered it towards Nathalie's neck.

The lids of her eyes were fluttering, but they were still closed.

Now. He had to do it now.

Jason hesitated.

Was he really going to do this?

He didn't have a choice. If he didn't end this now, the High Darkness would drag him into his office and spear him with his awful gaze. And then…

Not to mention the fact that Nathalie had gone renegade.

She had killed. She would kill again.

Jason was a daemon…but daemon's rarely killed. He himself never had. That was not their nature. To kill was…was to defeat the purpose, somehow.

She was a rabid dog. She had to be put down.

His hand trembled. He lowered the shadow towards her.

…But it was *Nathalie*. He had tricked her, tormented her, he had eaten part of her higher soul…

But he had loved her.

They had been partners, and he had loved her so much. It was so long ago. But laying there with her eyes closed, she looked the same as she had all those years ago, when they slumbered together, and the world turned lazily and…

Nathalie opened her eyes.

They were black as jet.

His hand tightened on the hilt of the knife, but it was too late.

With a roar, her arms shot out, and suddenly Jason was sailing backwards through the air.

He slammed through a thin plaster wall, then crashed into one of the thicker stone walls that formed the outside of the house. His wrist spasmed with the pain, and it was all he could do to keep his hold on the dagger.

She was so *strong*. Much stronger than she had been.

Stronger than him. Stronger by far.

He caught a glimpse of her face as he slid down the wall, saw the quirk of a smile, and then darkness was seething around her…

…and she was standing next to him.

His eyes widened, and he felt an explosion of mental energy burst from her.

To me!

She was shouting for help? Who could come to help her here?

He tried to bring the dagger down, but she caught his hand as easily as if it were a child's.

Then she was reaching out to him with her mind. The texture of her thoughts as they clawed and probed for him was so familiar. It had been so long since those days of togetherness. Even back then, before this, before everything, she had been so strong. A memory flashed through his mind. How they had lain together in the garden, in the sunshine, warm and happy and in love… how he had welcomed the touch of her mind, welcomed the sweet caress of her as she brushed against him, their thoughts entwining, every inch of him opened to her willingly…

No. That was then. He must not let her in.

He slammed his barriers down, felt her probing tendrils of thought flatten out against his shield. He must not let her pass. If she got into his mind…

Desperately, he tried to dissipate. His legs disappeared in a black mist, but she must have sensed what he was going to try before he even started, and her mind was ready, waiting for him. He felt her will snap forward and pull him back, blocking him from leaving.

She smiled.

Her head tilted, and he saw her black eyes turn inquisitively towards the dagger.

For just a single moment, her hold on him was broken. Jason put his feet to the wall and shoved. He summersaulted over her head. She snapped round with snake-speed to follow him, trying to keep the hold on his wrist…but he was moving a fraction too fast for her…

…And then they were no longer touching, and Jason dissipated.

But not to where she was expecting.

He was scared of her, of course he was.

She was a renegade. She was terrifying.

But you did not beat someone like that by being terrified. You beat them by being aggressive.

Jason rematerialized, leaping out of the wall he had just left. Her back was to him. She was still stretching her fingers vainly towards where he had been just a moment before, as if she could call back time.

The dagger was very cold in his hand.

It was pointing towards the back of her neck.

This was it. This was the moment he would kill her.

The blade was dark as midnight. It was death.

Jason turned the blade at the last possible second. He could not help himself.

Nathalie shrieked in pain as the shadow tore through the tissues of her shoulder, parting them as easily as if her bone and flesh and sinews were nothing, nothing at all.

Dark blood welled out of the wound. It splashed on the walls as Nathalie whirled around.

Her other arm swung out and hit him. Hard.

Jason crashed again into one of the thick stone walls of the house. This time it did not stop him, and he sailed out into the night.

He could not believe it. What had he done? Why had he hesitated?

THE FALL OF THE ANGEL NATHALIE

He was lying on damp, cold grass. He pulled himself up and looked desperately back to the house. Through the hole in the wall that had been carved by his passage, he caught a glimpse of Nathalie peering out at him.

Then her body was flashing into tendrils of darkness, and she was standing next to him again.

Blood was plastered on her shoulder, and she was giving the knife a wide berth. But she was smiling at him.

"You couldn't do it, could you?" she asked him conversationally. "After all this time, after all the things you have done…Still, you couldn't do this."

Jason licked his lips.

But she was right. He knew it with an awful, crushing certainty.

He couldn't kill her. He could never kill her.

"If I don't someone else will," he said. Was he telling her, or himself?

She shook her head, only slightly.

"They might try," she told him. "They are welcome to try."

Her head snapped up suddenly, and Jason realized people were approaching. He could hear their footsteps, could feel the vague luminescence of their minds. He frowned. There was something…something *strange* there. He could almost make it out…

All at once he perceived the gossamer tendrils of thought that hung between them and…

And Nathalie.

They were all connected to her. She had broken into their minds. What had she done to them?

They rushed in from all sides. There were…how many of them? Thirty? Forty?

He could not keep track of them all.

He felt commands shoot out from Nathalie and go darting through the ether towards her…her what? Her people? Her *slaves*?

And then they surrounded him.

Their bodies pressed in close. He could feel their warmth.

They were so young.

Some of them were only children. They stared at him. They were completely silent.

His gaze slipped over them, then back to her eyes.

"Go on," she told him. That horrible quirk of a smile was back on her face. "Go on. Try it. Kill me. I'll make it easy for you."

She strode forward, and her people parted for her like water, until she was standing close to him.

Only one body stood between them. He was a young boy, about ten or eleven Jason guessed. He was thin and gangly and his eyes were full of blind adoration.

Nathalie put her hands softly on the boy's shoulders, and sunk down until her head was directly behind his.

"All you have to do is drive that knife through the boy, and you will cut me, too," she told him. "It would be so easy. He wouldn't feel any pain, I could make sure of that."

Jason's eyes darted from Nathalie to the boy, and then back to Nathalie.

"Oh, yes, that's right," said Nathalie, as if she had suddenly remembered. "You can't, can you? You can't kill me, and you can't actually do anything to anyone. None of you can. Not really."

Her smile turned wicked.

"But I can," she told him simply. "I can. And so can they."

Suddenly Jason was hemmed in from all sides.

Her people were pushing him, trying to grab him, trying to pull him to the floor.

They looked wild. They looked crazy.

One of them, a young woman, tried to snatch the knife out of his hand. Startled, Jason pulled his arm up sharply, and the young woman was sent flying over his head. She landed in a heap on the ground.

He couldn't do this.

He had to be careful. If he killed just one of these humans, then…

Then he would be just like her.

He had to leave. His plan had not worked, and he needed to get away, to regroup.

He concentrated and made to pull the darkness to him, to vanish.

Something was stopping him.

He looked for Nathalie, but she was nowhere near him.

It was her people. The ones who were touching him. He could feel their minds, glaring at him, trying to pin him down, trying to hold him there.

Somehow, the thought strengthened him, made him angry.

He may have been defeated by a renegade. Maybe he had lost his nerve, maybe he had held back when he could have finished things.

But he was not going to be defeated by her toys.

With a roar, Jason lashed around. He was careful to keep something back, careful not to push with too much force. He could not afford to kill a single one of them. The people who held him were sent flying. He stood alone and untouched.

For a single instant they looked at one another, his yellow serpent's glare against the midnight black of her eyes.

"This is not over," he told her.

"Of course it isn't," she smiled back at him. "It's not over until I have won."

Jason called the darkness to him, and vanished into the vast night.

«««—»»»

Ben rolled as he hit the floor. He scrambled to his feet, but the man he had been clinging to had gone. He had vanished into thin air.

The feeling of overpowering hate that had swept him up, that had woken him from sleep and pulled him running to this house on the edge of town as fast as he could come, that urgent feeling faltered and faded away.

He was suddenly aware of his bare feet and the cuts and scratches up his legs.

He tried to think back, to remember why he had come, but it

was all a blur. He felt like he had scrambled through a thicket of brambles.

Looking around, he registered that he was not alone.

What the hell was going on?

Then a familiar hand was placed on his shoulders and he felt all his worries melt away.

Of course. It was so simple. He had come because he had been called. He had come as fast as he could, not caring for his stupid legs, his stupid flesh, because his mistress needed him. He had come to help—

—*and it's not right it's not right she's* using *you she's bending and tearing you and you can't do what she wants you have to fight you have to fight to fight to fight*—

—her, to make sure she was…

Ben staggered. A burst of pain shot through his head as if a bolt of lightning had just exploded in his brain.

Nathalie was standing over him now. She did not kneel down to help him.

Get up.

He heard the words echoing in his head as clearly as if she had spoken them in his ear.

He lifted one leg, and raised himself up on his knee. Oh God, the pain in his head…He felt like he was going to vomit. But that was no good. He could feel her will beating down on him, digging inside, wrenching his muscles and trying to make him stand. He clenched his eyes shut as tight as he could.

If only he could—

—*break free of her stop her stab her kill her break her before she breaks you and then you can make everything*—

—stop himself from vomiting, then he could stand up and he would please her and everything would be OK.

He retched, but nothing came up. He swallowed down big gulps of air and reached inside himself to find that hidden—*inner part*—of him that he knew somewhere was fighting and he

—*squashed*—

—it as flat as he could.

And the pain was gone. It was like a vacuum pump had been shoved inside his skull and sucked out all that red hot agony. It felt so good Ben started to cry.

And what did it matter if deep down inside he felt—

—*empty*—

—like a fool for crying in front of her? The pain was gone. That could only be good. Couldn't it?

He straightened up with ease.

Nathalie was smiling at him, and he returned the smile.

He loved her. She was so beautiful and good and she knew so much.

He knew he would do whatever she wanted, forever.

"Are you feeling better?" she asked him.

"Yes," he replied without hesitation. "I feel great. I feel wonderful. Only I'm…I'm sorry that he got away. That man. I'm sorry I let him go."

A jolt of revulsion washed through him. How could he have let her down so badly?

She saw what he was feeling, of course. When she brushed her hand against his cheek, he knew that everything was going to be OK. She had forgiven him. She loved him.

"What was that man trying to do?" he asked her.

"He wasn't a man," Nathalie corrected him. "That was one of the enemies I told you about. And he was trying to hurt me. To hurt us. He failed," she added, and Ben felt a stab of pride.

Of *course* he hadn't succeeded. How could anyone beat her? She was so powerful. She was justice itself.

Nathalie made a little *tsk* sound between her teeth.

"But he will be back," she told him. "Which means we need to be better. Better organized, better prepared…and stronger. We all need to be stronger…"

Nathalie trailed off, and when he looked up, those black eyes of hers were a million miles away.

She had thought of something. She had an idea.

"What is it?" he asked her.

It was so long before she answered him that Ben thought he wasn't going to get a reply.

"I need to teach you a new lesson," she said. "You, and a few others. The strongest amongst us, the ones with the most potential."

"What lesson?" Ben asked, but she just shook her head slowly.

"Just go and get some sleep for now," she said briskly, and Ben could tell that every one of the people nearby had heard her. "You need your strength for tomorrow's lesson. You might find it…difficult. But whatever doesn't kill us…"

She left the sentence hanging there, and began walking slowly towards the nearby house. She wasn't heading for the door—after all, it looked like there was a perfectly good hole in one of the walls that she could enter by.

Another lesson? What sort of a lesson?

"But…where are you going?" he asked, forlornly.

"Get to bed, Ben," she called back to him without turning her head. "I have to continue an interrupted conversation."

Then she was stepping inside the house. A moment later she was gone.

He yawned. Now that he thought about it, he felt bone tired.

He made his way across the lawn and back onto the road, slipping quietly into the stream of other people who were all walking listlessly back towards their homes.

He hadn't gone far before he heard the scream. It came from the house Nathalie had entered. It only lasted a fraction of a second, then it was cut off. Ben even thought he heard a faint crunching noise.

A frown flashed briefly across his face and for a horrible second he thought his headache was going to come back, but then—

—*nothing*—

—the feeling passed. He felt something wet trickling down the side of his face. He put one hand to his ear, and when he held it up to his eyes, there was blood on his fingers.

He told himself he didn't care.

Except for very, very deep down, he even believed it.

«‹‹—››»

Somewhere in the deep darkness a door swung open, and Jason stumbled out.

He did not know where he was. Daemonhearth was effectively endless, with millions upon millions of miles of potential space stretching out in every direction from the central region where the vast metropolis seethed. Not many daemons made their homes further out, though a few did.

Like many of his kind, Jason had at one point become fascinated with the dimensions of this strange world that dwelt below normal, human reality. Many, many years ago he had chosen a direction at random and set out, travelling as far as he could… or, rather, as far as he dared.

After a very long time, he had passed the areas that were merely sparsely inhabited, and had reached a region that was only half-real, that existed only because it had the potential to one day exist, if inhabitants brought portions of *real* with them and propped it up, stopped it from collapsing inwards.

It had felt thin there, thin and empty and awful; and when Jason had turned around to retrace his steps, it felt as if he was no longer able to get back to the centre, to the stinking, burning, *real* centre of the place. He had felt as if he were going mad, and after only a short time he was unable to tell how long he had been there, how long he had been trying to get back.

It had been one of the most awful, terrifying experiences of his long life, and when he somehow managed to finally claw his way back to an area that felt more thick, more real, he had sworn to himself that he would never stray into Daemonhearth except when he absolutely must. And he had kept his own vow. Even when he *did* have business that brought him there, he always stuck as close to the centre as he could. The thought of wandering off forever into those endless, thin, unreal passageways…

The place Jason was standing in now was not as thin as the far corner he had reached on that occasion, but he had a feeling it was close.

He knew why of course.

It was because, deep down, he did not want to get to the centre of Daemonhearth.

Not at all.

Because at the centre of Daemonhearth, someone was waiting for him...

But he had to go.

If he didn't go to the High Darkness, then the High Darkness would come to him.

He was sure of that much. Right now, the High Darkness was probably waiting for him. Maybe he even had an hourglass on his desk. Maybe the sand was already running thin...

Jason had no doubt at all that the High Darkness knew of his failure. Everyone reported to the High Darkness. Information like this would never have passed him by.

So Jason had no choice.

He forced himself to step back into the gateway he had opened, and shut it behind him.

He hung in the emptiness. He forced himself to concentrate.

He opened the gateway again, and stepped out.

He stood in front of the large, plain door. It was open.

The High Darkness was waiting for him.

He stepped forward, and stopped in the doorway. The High Darkness stood there, looking at him.

He was not alone. And Jason knew the other figure who stood there. He seemed to fill the room, dominating it. Next to that one, even the High Darkness seemed diminished.

Jason stood in the doorway, gazing warily at the figure. He had not seen him for over three hundred years. He looked exactly the same. His hair was silver-grey, his eyes were cold blue.

And his wings were white as snow.

"Come in Jason," the High Darkness commanded, and Jason complied. What choice did he have?

The door swung shut behind him. The room felt very close.

"I think you know my, ah, guest," said the High Darkness pleasantly.

Jason looked Aekmar in the eyes for a moment. A moment was all he could manage.

"Yes, I do," Jason said, a slight strain in his voice. He licked his lips. "We used to know each other quite well."

The angel did not show any flicker of recognition. His face was stony cold and still.

"I understand that you did," said the High Darkness. "I also understand that you have failed in your task."

Jason opened his mouth to explain, but the High Darkness cut him off with a gesture.

"When I found that out, I was rather displeased," he told Jason gently. "As I am sure you can imagine. I realized that I had obviously given you a bigger job than you could handle. No, don't say anything. Your actions speak very clearly for themselves."

The High Darkness looked at him with lazy, half-lidded eyes.

"I then decided that if you could not deal with our little, ah, embarrassment," he went on, "that it was my duty to issue an official warning to the Higher Authorities. Hence, our respected guest."

Here the High Darkness gestured elaborately towards the angel.

Jason frowned as he tried to understand what he was being told.

The Higher Authorities were getting involved? But that meant that the High Darkness would not be giving him another chance. And if he didn't get another chance, then *that* meant…

"I can still do it," Jason surprised himself by choking out. That hurt. He thought his begging days were well and truly behind him. Oh well, why stop when you're on a role…

"I can do it," he repeated, "I made a mistake before. I…I hesitated. It was stupid. It…it won't happen next time."

The High Darkness was looking at him with interest.

"You know, Jason," he said conversationally, "there are not many of my people who would dare interrupt me as you have just done. In another context, I might take it as bravery. Of course, in your case, it is not bravery but simple, blind desperation. You know very well what I will do to you now that you have failed."

Jason took a breath, but this time it was the angel who spoke over him.

"I have no patience for this," said Aekmar, still not looking at Jason. "I have explained our position. Surely you cannot have been surprised? The Higher Authorities will not intervene. We cannot do so, even now. She is one of your people, and it is your people who will pay the price if she is not brought to heel."

For the first time that Jason could remember, the High Darkness looked angry. It was only for an instant, and then that smooth mask was back in place...but it had been there.

"Jason," he snapped. "Tell him what you saw. What you saw her doing with your own eyes."

Jason was so dizzy with relief that at first he could not speak.

So the Higher Authorities were not doing anything.

Of course they weren't. When had they ever? That went against their most fundamental principle: free will.

People had to make their own choices, clean up their own messes, or pay the consequences. Even when the people in question happened to be daemons...

If there was not to be an Intervention, then surely he would be given another chance. He was sure of it.

You won't be able to do it, some traitor part of his soul screamed. *You failed once because of what she used to mean to you. What makes you think you will succeed if you are given another chance?*

Jason swallowed, and pushed the thought away.

"Well, daemon?" asked Aekmar, his blue eyes peering intently at Jason. "I am waiting."

Jason took a breath.

"She was very powerful," Jason said, trying to keep his voice as flat as possible. "More powerful than I thought was possible. She has…she has been killing. She continues to kill. She is using the souls of those she kills in this way to increase her strength. And she has followers. She is controlling them."

"There!" exclaimed the High Darkness. "Did I not tell you?" He turned his hands towards Aekmar, imploring. "She is passing out of our control. She is committing Intervention upon Intervention. You are telling me that you will do nothing to stop her? When human lives are in the balance? When she is breaking and trampling the rules herself, you will hold so tightly to them? And if you will not think of them, then what of her? I was given to understand that she was your friend. I thought you would at least *try* to save her!"

Aekmar looked unmoved.

"That is *precisely* when we will hold most tightly to our rules, naturally," the angel said in an even voice. "Otherwise, what are we? Our decision not to intercede despite our power to do so is everything we stand for. And in any case," he added, drawing himself up. "You cannot believe you are telling us something we did not already know? We have been watching her most carefully. Ever since she became one of yours, ever since she…" he glanced at Jason, "…fell. She was powerful, and she was wise. She was my friend. But she is gone, and what remains is nothing but her… her shadow. She cannot be saved. It has been too late for that since the beginning." Aekmar looked at the High Darkness with a sad smile on his face. "Did you think it was just yourselves and the daemons who are being judged? We all have a bar against which we are measured, and some of us are found wanting."

Aekmar took a step closer to the High Darkness. With every step he seemed to grow. His wings seemed to fill the whole room.

"And do not *dare* to insult me by mentioning the human cost!" Aekmar's voice was quiet, but there was an awful heaviness to his words. "You know as well as I do that those who die by her hand are granted another turn of the wheel. And we know very well why you are so eager to get rid of her. Tell me, how many little trophies has she stolen from your kind with her handing out of clean slates?"

The High Darkness was very still. He did not answer.

Aekmar glared at him for a moment, then leaned back. He seemed to draw into himself again.

"You have made your petition, and you have your answer," he said coldly. "You will have no more of my time. May I suggest that you stop wasting yours, too, and get on with the business of cleaning up your mess."

Then Aekamar was gone.

There was no flash of light, no feeling of movement. He was simply gone.

Jason was alone with the High Darkness.

He opened his mouth to speak.

"You have a day," said the High Darkness, very quietly. "One day. Twenty four hours. Put her down, or I will have to. You will not get a further chance. Now get out."

Jason knew better than to say another word.

He had been given a reprieve. He had been given a second chance.

He closed the door behind him when he left.

And you will fail this time, too, spoke up the traitor part of him again.

It was true. He had to face it, or it was as good as over.

He would hesitate again. He would not strike the blow.

How could he kill her when he could not bring himself to land the blow? It was hopeless.

Unless…

Yes. Yes, that might work.

No, part of him screamed, the same part of him that had hesitated, the same part of him that still…what, that still loved her? Was that even possible?

He pushed the thought away.

She had to be destroyed. If she was not destroyed, then he would be.

And if he could not be trusted to deal the death-blow…Well, he needed help, didn't he?

And he knew someone who would just jump at the chance.

THE FALL OF THE ANGEL NATHALIE

«‹‹—››»

The sun was half way across the sky before Ben felt he had the hang of it, but Nathalie was still patient with him.

She was patient with all ten of them, all ten of her star recruits got smiles and encouragement and that special, warm feeling inside when they did it just right.

Not to mention the power.

Now that felt so good, all on its own. Ben knew not a drop of *that* feeling was coming from Nathalie. Even though no one had done it cleanly yet, they all felt the reflected power when one of them came close.

There were only the two retirement homes in the town, and at first, when it seemed that none of them were making any progress, that none of them were getting it right, Ben had wondered if it would be enough. After all, it was such a narrow window. He couldn't even *see* it the first couple of times she showed them. That had made him feel so stupid. To begin with, he had thought Nathalie would make them go out in the bus to some of the neighbouring towns, practice on the old folks over there.

But then the girl with the yellow hair had screamed, "I see! I see it!" excitedly, just a fraction of a second after Nathalie had made the sharp twisting motion with her hand.

And Ben had thought he saw something, too.

Only he had been distracted because the old man's foot had started jerking when Nathalie had snapped his neck, and it had kicked Ben right in the belly.

The next time, over half of them had seen it.

It was like a…like a shimmering glow, only you didn't see it with your eyes. Instead, you had to be reaching out with your mind. If you touched their thoughts at the exact moment their life was extinguished, you could sort of *see* the…well, the essence, he supposed, as it leaked out of the body and drifted away.

And if you were very quick, you could catch it.

At first, Ben had felt uncomfortable about what they were doing. He wasn't sure why, because Nathalie had explained it all to them. How these people were sinners—just because someone was old did not mean they were harmless, even he knew that. But it wasn't just that. It was because they were the chosen ones. They were the ones who were going to make a difference. They were the ones who were going to heal the world.

And to do that they had to be strong.

The old people understood, Nathalie told them all. She made sure of that. She made sure they did not suffer. They knew that they were giving up their lives so that Nathalie's lieutenants could gain strength…When they knew that, Nathalie said, the old people would willingly lay down their lives.

And she was right. Mostly, the old people had stepped forward unflinchingly. Some even seemed eager. And the one or two who didn't, who tried feebly to force Nathalie away as she stood over them and calmly reached for their necks…well, that just proved those ones had something to feel guilty for, didn't it?

"Focus, Ben," Nathalie told him, watching him intently with those kind black eyes of her.

"Sorry," said Ben. He snapped his mind back to the present.

"I know you can do this, sweetie," Nathalie encouraged him. "Remember. Just like you did before. You did brilliantly with the last one. You almost drank it all. I *know* you can get it all this time. Every last drop."

Ben nodded, and focussed on his breathing.

He could do this. He would do this for her, for his mistress.

"Now…hold her mind," Nathalie told him.

Ben looked at Mrs. Lee.

He remembered her from when he was very small. She had sometimes helped out at the kindergarten when he was little. She used to smile at him. She had been very active for her age. That had been before her stroke, of course, but still…

Now her eyes were rolled back in her head. Ben reached out for her mind, and he could feel the weight of Nathalie's thoughts bearing down on the old woman, keeping her still, keeping her from squirming.

"Ready?" said Nathalie softly.

Ben nodded. Nathalie moved her hand. There was a low cracking sound.

Ben forgot to breathe, he was concentrating so hard.

He felt Mrs.'s Lee's mind spasm and shake. It did not understand what was happening, and he felt a vague feeling of confusion, of disappointment wash back through the connection towards him.

Then her mind was shrinking, drawing back into itself, drying up and dying away into nothing. And then...

...And then he felt the *shimmering* as the mind he had been touching turned inwards on itself, and shook away the dead body which had been its home for so many years. It drifted upwards, a glimmering, translucent lightness. It was beautiful.

"Now!" said Nathalie, but he was already moving.

His thoughts streamed out, and grasped the translucent thing. He felt it tremble powerlessly, like a tiny embryo fighting an abortion.

Then he sucked it back into himself.

The thing was gone...

...And the *light* that blossomed within him was nirvana.

It seemed to go on forever. He could have been floating there for a million years.

After what seemed like an age, the feeling receded.

He opened his eyes.

The whole group was looking at him. They were all smiling, but Nathalie's smile was the most beautiful.

"You did it!" she told him, and kissed him very lightly on one cheek.

Everyone in the circle clapped, and Ben felt—

—*disgust*—

—pride rise in him. He thought it was the proudest he had ever been.

"You see!" Nathalie told them all, when the applause had died down. "You can all do this! That was why I chose you. You all have it in you. And the more you do it, the easier it will become. Because the more you do it, the more powerful you will be."

The little coterie looked at one another. This felt so *good*. This felt so *right*.

"Now," said Nathalie, "who's next?"

It went on like that all day, and by early evening, they could all do what Nathalie had taught them, and cleanly, too.

Ben walked beside Nathalie as they left the residential home. He felt about a million miles tall. It was as if he had been running on empty his whole life, and it was only now that he knew what it felt like to have a full tank. He felt like he could leap over mountains. Just by thinking about it, he could feel what pretty much anyone else in the town was up to. He hardly even had to try.

For some reason, his mind wandered briefly back to how Mrs. Lee had looked as they left the room, small and alone and sad, and—

—and he cut the thought off before it could form and give him a headache.

No.

Why did he keep thinking things like that? He should know by now it wouldn't do him any good.

Instead, he looked up at Nathalie, and asked her a question.

"So are we ready now?" he said.

"Ready for what?" she replied.

"Ready for the bad man," he answered. "In case he comes back again. You said he was coming back again, remember? You said we had to be ready for him."

Nathalie was nodding.

"We're ready for him, I think," she told Ben. "But still. I want to make sure."

Sure? How could they be any more sure? If the man in the suit came back, Ben felt like he could take him on his own. Why did he need to do anymore...anymore—

—charging himself up?

"How are we going to do that?" his voice sounded thin suddenly, but it did not seem as if Nathalie had noticed.

"Don't worry," she told him. "I'll explain it all at the town meeting tonight. At the church. Everyone will be there. I'll make sure of that. Meanwhile, I have one more little errand to run."

Ben nodded his understanding, but already she was gone.

His ear was wet again. He had managed to push the headache away, somehow—maybe it was because he was so filled up with power—but it looked like he couldn't stop the bleeding. It had happened two times already this day. He was pretty sure he had managed to clear the blood away before Nathalie had noticed.

Why did that seem so important?

He wasn't sure. But for some reason, some deep part of him felt—*knew*—that it was vital that none of the others had noticed.

He pulled a handkerchief out of his pocket. It was matted with dark, dry blood.

He cleaned his ear as best he could, then made his way back home to see his mother.

A town meeting, huh?

And the whole town would be there. Him and the other nine that Nathalie had chosen. And everyone else.

He wondered vaguely what Nathalie would tell them.

«««—»»»

In his dream, he got there in time.

In his dream, he told her, no, wait. I love you.

I love you. Don't do it. Whatever it is you do to yourself: just don't do it.

In his dream, she listened to him. She told him she loved him, too.

Then they left and they never came back. Not ever.

Blake smiled in his sleep. He knew that he was dreaming, somewhere deep down inside.

Still.

Who wouldn't choose the dream? When the reality was this, who would want to wake up?

The air shifted in his cell.

He woke up. He didn't have a choice.

Jason was standing in front of him. He opened his mouth to tell him where to go…and closed it again. Something was different.

Blake peered at the figure. His suit looked crumpled. And his sunglasses were gone. His eyes glittered yellow in the darkness. But that wasn't everything…

"Where's that sarcastic, shit-eating smile of yours?" Blake asked him, neutrally.

Ray was sleeping on the bottom bunk, but he didn't bother to lower his voice. Frankly, he didn't really give much of a damn anymore.

The figure didn't say anything, and just for a moment Blake wondered if he had made a mistake, if he was still half-asleep and imaging the yellow eyes, that it was really Kain who had snuck into his cell. Maybe that was it. Maybe he would pin him down and smother him with a pillow.

He found he didn't really care too much one way or the other.

Then the figure moved closer, and Blake was sure he had been right the first time. He wasn't still dreaming, it was definitely the daemon.

"I'm going to offer you her death," Jason said simply, and Blake felt something icy begin to slide down his spine. "Come with me, now, tonight, and she is yours."

Blake tried to keep his heart from hammering his chest to pieces. He swung his legs over the side of the bunk, forcing himself to be slow, and jumped easily down to the floor.

He slid next to Jason. Up close, he could see that the daemon did not look in very good shape. His face was covered in cuts and bruises, and there was something about his eyes…

Blake struggled to put his finger on it, then realized what it was.

"You look defeated," he told Jason flatly.

Jason raised one hand gently as if to say, *yeah, so what?*

Blake licked his lips, thinking.

Was this a trick? How could he, a human, kill Nathalie, who was a…who was a, well, whatever she was?

That was it. It must be a trick. Jason had simply read him, simply worked out what the only thing was that he really wanted, the only thing with which he could tempt him.

And yet…

187

And yet there was something in the daemon's appearance, in his whole demeanor which screamed that he was telling the truth. There was nothing flashy in him anymore. He seemed to simply be telling him the truth, and he could take it or leave it.

"How?" he asked at length. Then he thought for a moment, and added, "And why? Why me?"

Jason dropped his eyes before he answered him, and that was when Blake realized he believed him, one hundred percent, no more questions asked.

"Because I can't," the daemon told him simply. "I've tried, and I can't. Because I still love her. Which sounds crazy, coming from me, I know. But it's true. And because she *needs* to be killed," Jason added, looking straight at him. It was the only time Blake could ever remember the daemon sounding earnest.

Blake shrugged.

That made some kind of sense, actually. To him it did.

"OK," he said. "How?"

Then Jason showed him the knife, and Blake felt the last of his doubts vanish.

He didn't know what it was, but this thing *oozed* danger. It seemed to make the dark cell even darker.

He licked his lips.

"Yes," he said.

Jason nodded, and moved closer. Blake saw tendrils of darkness begin to weave themselves around them both, and realized that Jason was getting ready to dissipate them out of the prison.

But no. Not yet. He had a couple of loose threads to tie up first.

"Wait," he said. Jason shot him an irritated glance, but the tendrils of darkness dropped away.

He lifted his mattress and extracted his meagre supply of money. He would not be needing money again, he realized.

He leant down to tuck it under Ray's blanket, and saw there were two eyes staring up at him, huge and white and terrified.

He hesitated for a moment, then laid the money on his cellmate's chest.

"I'm sure you didn't see anything," he told him. "I'm sure you just woke up, and I'd picked the lock and gone. I didn't wake you."

Ray didn't say a word, but Blake saw those big white eyes bob up and down urgently.

One down, one to go.

"Unlock the door, please," he told Jason.

The daemon shook his head slightly, but he gestured sharply and the cell door made a small clicking noise.

Blake tried it, and it slid smoothly back.

He walked out of the cell. He felt more than heard the daemon fall into step behind him.

As he trod silently past row upon row of metal bars, he felt the balance of the dagger Jason had given him. It was perfect.

He moved neither fast nor slow. He did not look for guards, or listen for footsteps other than his own. He felt sure Jason would ensure there were no further interruptions.

He came to the cell he wanted. He hadn't realized his brain had stored the information, but this was it, he had known where to come, after all.

He lifted the knife. A shaft of moonlight falling from a window high above them lit the handle in a silver halo, but did not touch the blade. He raked it along the row of metal bars, and felt no resistance, none at all. The blade passed through the metal as if the bars were not even there. He made another sweep, lower, and the transected bars fell out one by one and clattered to the floor.

It was loud, but Blake didn't care.

To his credit, Kain was up and out of the bed before Blake was even inside the cell.

Not that it did him any good.

At first he sounded angry, but it wasn't long before the shouts were shouts of pain and terror.

Blake didn't say anything, but he remembered that he had been kicked and punched many, many times, and he felt sure that Kain had used both his left and his right hand.

He wasn't quite as certain when it came to the kicks, so he decided to leave the man his left foot.

After all, he wasn't a monster, was he?

"Happy now?" Jason asked him as he came out of the cell. He wasn't sure, but it looked like there was a quirk of a smile on the daemon's face. Perhaps he was getting his sense of humor back.

The screaming was very loud, and lights were starting to come on somewhere further off in the huge warren of cells. People were shouting. Footsteps were coming.

"Not happy," Blake told him, "just even."

"Good," Jason said.

Then the darkness was rushing around them, and the prison was gone.

«‹‹—›››

There were lots of high fences here, but they didn't matter.

There were several turrets, each one had machine gun emplacements on top, and were manned by a minimum of two soldiers each, at any one time.

That didn't matter either.

The place Nathalie needed to get to was thirty metres underground, and the entrance was blocked by a steel door that was three feet thick and controlled by various high-tech security devices that made unauthorized entry very, very difficult to the average would-be intruder.

They did not impede Nathalie in the slightest, of course.

There was a soldier posted behind the door. He was the lucky one. Nathalie was able to dissipate so far past him that he didn't even hear anything and had no idea that anything was amiss until he received the frantic telephone call exactly ninety seconds later.

The soldier who was posted just outside the room Nathalie wanted to get to had a much better idea that something was amiss.

He had time to say, "Hey, what do…?"

Then there was a soft, wet noise and everything was silent.

Nathalie felt a momentary twinge as she stepped over the body. The poor guy hadn't been especially bad. He probably hadn't shot anyone, maybe he hadn't even ever beaten anyone up. Perhaps he even gave money to charity and slowed down to keep from running over stray animals.

But then, he was in her way.

And her way was the right way.

If time had not been an issue, maybe she would have indulged herself and educated the man.

But she could already feel the clock ticking.

Jason would be coming back. She knew it. How could he not?

The angels had their stupid, stifling laws of non-Intervention, and it was highly unlikely they would ever lift a finger to stop her, unless the stakes were very grave indeed.

But the daemons...

They would not like what she had been doing. Not one bit. There was no way they could leave her to build her little empire, to steal their victories out from under them. They would try something. They would try something soon. And if they won...well, the world was doomed. It was obvious. The single, brilliant beacon of light she was attempting to set up like a flare for all of humanity to see would be snuffed out before it had properly been lit.

She could not allow that to happen.

No, the attack would come soon. And when it did...

She would be ready for them.

Nathalie stepped into the inner chamber and looked around her.

Rack upon rack of dark metal shined back.

But it wasn't the metal objects she was after. They were very common after all.

There were probably thirty or forty guns in her town anyway. She could have used them, but then there was the problem of synchronisation...

She walked deeper in.

The objects that lined the wall were no longer black, they were mostly grey.

She surveyed them for a moment, then selected one and stooped to pick it up.

It wasn't the biggest, not by far, though it was heavy. But then, it wasn't a very big town. It wouldn't have to be big.

Somewhere far off, a warning light began to flash.

Nathalie smiled. Now all she had to do was tell her disciples what was expected of them.

They had all proved themselves quite adept at their little task earlier that day, she was sure they could manage what she required.

It might be the case that the daemons would only be sending their minor servants to deal with her for now, but she had no doubt that as she continued to defy them, and as they understood more clearly how big a threat she was, that they would take her more seriously.

She needed soldiers badly if she was going to prevail at that point.

Not just soldiers. *Strong* soldiers.

And soon she would have them.

She called the darkness to her and vanished with her package.

«««—»»»

"You want me to drink *what*?" spluttered Blake sounding out-raged.

Jason sighed theatrically, put a hand to his brow.

He had begun to feel a bit more like his normal self. He was even wearing his sunglasses again.

"Look, I was the one who tempted them," he said patiently. "I'm the one who collected them. It's not like you will have done anything wrong."

Blake looked at him through narrowed eyes.

"Except that I would have drunk someone's *soul*," he said emphatically.

"What's the problem, are you a vegetarian?"

"No!" Blake nearly shouted. "But I'm not a bloody cannibal, either!"

192

Jason tilted his head as if to say, *fine, suit yourself.*

Then he lowered the vial he had been offering the young man, opened it, and drained the soul he had harvested countless years before.

That was better. He felt almost restored now…

Blake had not been happy when Jason had explained they needed to make a minor detour before going to find the woman he wanted to kill; but then, Jason was damned if he was going into battle without his battery charged to full, and he had told him as much.

"You *are* damned," Blake had reminded him, which had been a fair point.

Jason replaced the empty vials in the white container that housed his collection. He hesitated, unsure if it would be wise to take any further charged vials with him, in case he needed rejuvenating once their mission was underway.

But I already do *have one vial with me,* he suddenly realized.

His hand went to his breast pocket before he could stop himself.

What remained of her soul. He had had it with him all this time. He could have consumed that when he was fighting her last time. Now why hadn't he thought of that? It might even have tipped the balance…

The thought made him uncomfortable. He pushed the feeling down, and turned back to Blake.

"Are you sure you don't want one?" he asked. "Some of them are really delicious. Not to mention that they would give you a real energy boost, which is the main point. Are you sure I can't, ah, tempt you?"

Blake shook his head.

"You've already given me all I need to kill her," said Blake, and the certainty in his voice made Jason blink. "Just take me to her. Just take me to her, and I'll do the rest."

Jason shrugged. He reached out with his mind and pulled the darkness around them.

Then they were standing on rough cobblestones in the centre of a crowd of onlookers.

A collective gasp went up from the gathered spectators. Jason made an elaborate bow. Then he turned to a man on a unicycle who was juggling knives. The man had a rather angry look on his face.

"Sorry," Jason told him, sounding not a bit of it. "Must have got my times muddled up. Didn't mean to steal your thunder."

Then he bowed to the thunderstruck audience one more time, and led the bemused Blake away down a side-street. The crowd gave them another round of applause as they walked away.

"Of course, I could have dissipated up into the toilets or something, but where would the fun be in that?" Jason said. "I've always loved Covent Garden. Great place to pick up clients. Full of drunks and hippies. And people looking for un-usual things that they can't buy in the high street shops. And best of all, there's lots and lots of storage space underneath the boule-vards. Has been for hundreds of years. The traders use it for their stock."

He shrugged.

"After all, I'm a trader, too," he said. "In fact, I even experi-mented with having a stall of my own, once…"

"I don't care," Blake told him, coldly. "You said we were in a hurry. Making yourself ready for a fight, that I can understand. But you've done that, and we're still standing here. What are we waiting for?"

Jason shrugged.

"You're right," he said. "Just thought you might want to see London one last time. You do know that if you don't kill her, then it's almost certain she'll kill us both, right?"

"She already did," said Blake.

"Oh, stop being such a fucking *goth*!" said Jason, rolling his eyes.

Blake stared at him flatly.

To his surprise, Jason found that he was the one who couldn't hold the gaze.

Blake came closer, and for a single moment, Jason actually thought that the young man was going to pull the blade on him.

But Blake's hands remained in his pockets; and when he spoke, his voice was soft.

"You told me you loved her," Blake said to him. "How much?"

To his own surprise, Jason found that he answered honestly.

"A lot," he said. "More than anything. More than anyone." He paused. "More than myself," he added.

Blake nodded, as if that was what he had been expecting.

"And you lost her," he said. It wasn't a question.

Jason licked his lips.

"I lost her," he answered.

Had it been that he had lost her? Or was it more correct to say that she had lost him?

It didn't matter. Not really. Ether way, they had lost each other.

"And whose fault was it?" Blake asked. "Whose fault was it that you lost her?"

Jason didn't hesitate for a moment. What was the point in lying, anyway?

"Mine," he told the young man. "Mine, of course."

Blake nodded again.

"And how did that make you feel?"

"Stupid," said Jason. "Stupid, and worthless. And angry, of course."

"Angry," agreed Blake. "And those other things, too. That's how I felt, when Nathalie took Laura from me. And it was like those things—the anger, the shame, the darkness—those were the only things that were left of me. My life was destroyed, it was over, it was ripped to pieces. And all that was left was a huge, ragged scar where my life used to be. And it filled up with those feelings, like blood seeping up into an open wound.

"So I'm not joking when I say she killed me," Blake went on. "I'm not being melodramatic. I'm telling you how things are. And I know you understand me, because I know you felt the same way, too, when you lost the woman you love. There's two differences between us, Jason. The first is that it was your fault you lost Nathalie, and it wasn't my fault I lost Laura. The second," he added, leaning forward and whispering into Jason's ear, "is that I know when I'm dead."

Blake leaned backwards and looked away.

I can think of another difference, Jason thought. But he didn't say it.

Instead he shrugged.

"Well, I don't know about you, but I feel much better about myself now," he said. "Talking really is the answer, isn't it?"

Blake just looked at the ground.

Jason sighed.

"Come on," he said. "Let's go and kill my ex-girlfriend."

He wished he was as confident as he sounded.

The darkness pulled inwards, and Covent Garden was gone.

«« —»»

The sun had set thirty minutes ago, but Ben wasn't cold in the slightest. Even though the wind that blew over his head and ruffled his hair was cold and had teeth, he welcomed it gladly.

Imagine what it must be like inside, he thought, but decided not to.

It was uncomfortable enough here, in the grounds outside the church. Inside, with people packed from wall to wall and not the faintest gust of wind to cool them, it must be stifling.

People were packed tight enough where he was, in a dense crowd outside the main entrance; and more kept coming, too. He could feel their minds as they approached, little pinpricks of light drifting out of the dark streets of the town and coalescing with the bright mass of souls gathered around the church.

He could almost make out their individual thoughts. He barely had to concentrate anymore.

Ever since the "training" session that morning, his brain was sparking and purring away like a fancy car engine that had been treated to a premier-class service. Thoughts seemed to flash around in lightning bursts of insight. He even thought he might be able to read what Nathalie was thinking if he wanted to...

He stopped the thought before it was fully formed.

That thought would lead to other thoughts and—

—when she comes you can look in her mind and if you're right if your guess was right if she's going to come and—

—no good could come of that.

His eyes swam for a moment with the effort of blocking himself, and then he suddenly realized he was staring at Tara Hagan, one of the folks they had picked up in the city. She smiled at him, and he felt a flare of warmth open up in her. He smiled back. He couldn't help it. Tara was pretty and smart and—

—and she killed people earlier just like you did and—

—very talented. Nathalie had obviously been impressed with her. She was probably the most apt pupil out of all of them.

Except for Ben himself, that was.

"Hi, Tara," Ben said.

"Hi," she replied. "Do you know when, uh, when she's getting here?"

Ben shook his head.

"No," he told her. "But I don't think it'll be long. I think…"

But then he felt her, and it was no longer necessary to speak anymore.

It was almost as if the world lurched around him. He knew without looking at her that Tara felt it, too. A moment before, Nathalie had not been there. The next, she was perched on top of the church steeple, looking down on them.

Ben felt as if he were an iron filing on a tray onto which a strong magnet had just been dropped. He felt her appear. It was like the sun coming out from behind the clouds.

Nathalie gazed down at them for a long moment. The crowd hushed. Silence stretched.

"My good people, the time has come," Nathalie said at last, and though her voice was not loud, Ben had no doubt that every single person gathered there heard her as clearly as if she were whispering in their ear.

"You have all been waiting for so very, very long," she went on. "Most of you have been waiting all your lives. Didn't we all

197

believe that when we grew up, we could make this world a better place? That we would avoid the mistakes, the greed, the ugly things we saw the adults doing? Today, that day has come. Today we take the first step towards challenging evil…"

There was a seething of darkness around Nathalie, and she vanished, only to emerge a moment later striding out of the doors of the church, with tendrils of black cloying to her arms and legs.

"…And force it to melt away to nothing," she completed.

She glanced around the gathered crowd. They stared at her in adoration.

She caught Ben's eye, and smiled, and it was as if her eyes were burning into his soul.

She was so beautiful and so warm and wise and—

—she knows she knows she knows and she'll burn me with those eyes and—

—she looked away.

"All of you can take part in this," Nathalie said, her voice rising. "Tonight is the night we all stand up and be counted! Tonight is the night we TAKE OUR WORLD BACK!"

Ben felt a wave of euphoria sweep out from Nathalie, felt it lift him up as helplessly as if he were a leaf being bobbed around on a tidal wave. He felt it smash into the crowd, and suddenly everyone was screaming, shouting, baying like wild, joyful animals.

He was doing the same. He couldn't help himself.

The wave of joy began to recede, and then he felt it: the command to go inwards, to push ever inwards into the church.

It didn't touch him. No, it wasn't him that was being forced to go inside.

It was the crowd, everyone else, with the exception of Nathalie's ten lieutenants, of course.

People had been forced in tight before, but there must have been more room, somehow, because the wooden parapet of the church was shaking as feet marched over it, and bodies were disappearing inside.

They must be piling up three deep in there, Ben thought. And somewhere, deep down inside, he felt an awful dread begin to creep and stir.

And then the call was coming for him. He felt the focus of Nathalie's power shift, and suddenly his feet were moving. Out of the corner of his eye, he could see the other lieutenants moving, too. They were not going towards the church, and they were not going in the same direction, either. Instead, they were spreading outwards, forming a ragged circle with the church fifty or a hundred metres away at the centre.

Experimentally, he tried to stop himself from moving, but it was no good, and he quickly gave up before he—

—drew attention to—

—hurt himself.

He looked again, watching impassively as himself and the other lieutenants marched away in perfect step.

As if they were soldiers…or puppets.

«« —»»

For the second time in twenty-four hours, the Atlantic skimmed by below Jason. Only this time, he was not alone.

He had to be careful to not go so high that Blake passed out from lack of oxygen, or get to a point where the air was so thin that the air friction—when they re-entered it—would burn him up. If they accelerated to too great a free-fall velocity, it would be a one-way process. Even though they had stopped to steal the young man a parachute, he would only stay alive to use it if his fall was limited to a non-terminal velocity.

Not long now, Jason told himself.

Soon it will be over. One way or another.

He wrapped his arms tighter around Blake, and made another jump.

Before long, the East coast of America swam into sight.

It was a clear night, and the stars were coming out.

It would be cold.

THE FALL OF THE ANGEL NATHALIE

«‹‹—›››

Ben heard the purring of an engine pull up somewhere behind him, but he couldn't even turn around to look. He could feel the weight of Nathalie's mind on him, crushing down on his shoulders, cramping every muscle in his body.

He was as powerless to move as if she were standing behind him, locking him in place.

There was a hissing sound as a hydraulic door opened, and Ben realized it was the school bus. It was disgorging the last few inhabitants of the town. He felt their minds drift gently into the pulsating mass of dominated thought that was concentrating itself tighter and tighter into the church.

He felt like a single instrument in a vast orchestra, with Nathalie as the conductor. He could feel the ghosting of her thoughts as they surged out from her in all directions, calling out to people, forcing them to push closer in, bearing down on them. It was sweet and cloying and completely unstoppable.

The stars twinkled overhead. The wind was picking up.

For some reason, it seemed to carry the scent of the ocean.

«‹‹—›››

And then the town was below them, directly below them, and Jason knew the time had come. He could feel the tug of her mind. It was like a dark magnet, sucking everything inwards.

Jason frowned. Her mind was not alone. He could feel the weight of countless human thoughts surging and beating below him. They were concentrated thicker and stronger than they had any right to be. It was entirely unlike the background hum of human minds, which pulsed and heaved and pulled in a thousand directions at once.

No, this mass of thought was beating in concert, somehow. It was as if every mind, every single mind had been...

...Had been polarized.

That was it, he suddenly realized. The human minds had been

exposed to a great magnet. All the particles of consciousness had run together, arranging themselves along the lines of force that echoed out from that dark power.

The arc of their flight faded away; Jason and Blake began to fall straight down.

She's too strong, Jason thought wildly. *Maybe I can hold off her assaults…but Blake?*

There was no way. The moment she sensed the young man, he would be overcome, and then Jason would have one more human puppet to fight.

Only this human puppet would have an absolutely deadly weapon…

Desperately, Jason constructed barrier after barrier of psychic material, and layered it around Blake's mind. It was like a mass of spider-silk, and Jason wove it as strong and as tight as he dared. Too much, and he might interfere with Blake's ability to act. And if he did that…well, then Nathalie wouldn't be the only one guilty of Intervention…

The town swelled beneath them. The white spire of the church jutted up out of the darkness, pointing at them like an accusing finger.

A church, Jason had time to think. *How apt.*

Then they were out of time. He reached around to the pack Blake wore on his back and grasped the handle.

"Remember not to hesitate," he told the young man, but he knew it was unnecessary advice.

Blake wouldn't hesitate. As long as Jason gave him the chance, Nathalie was as good as dead.

Jason pulled the parachute chord. Blake jerked and was pulled upwards, and Jason was falling alone.

«««—»»»

"Eyes up," Nathalie commanded, and Ben had no choice.

His neck tilted, and his eyes were pointed up into the sky. He felt a strengthening of the bond between him and Nathalie, and

201

a moment later, he felt an echo of that bond shooting out between her and the other nine of her chosen.

He could see through their eyes, just as he was sure they could see through his.

It was incredible. It was beautiful and spectacular and it felt like his mind was going to melt.

Then his eyes were drawn to where Nathalie's mind was pointing, and with a desperate creak, the last of his resistance gave way.

He wasn't Ben anymore, not really.

He was an extension of her. A great sense of peace overcame him

All was well. All was as it should be. All was going as s/he had foreseen.

«««—»»»

A few moments before Jason hit her, he realized he had miscalculated, and he tried to pull back.

But he could not dissipate. He could not pull his body back into the darkness.

There was a wall of mental energy blocking him. It was coming from Nathalie, but that wasn't the true source, at least, not of all the power.

He flailed desperately with his mind, trying to understand what was happening, trying to unlock the web that was fastening him in place.

It was her followers. He could feel them arranged around the church, arranged in a perfect circle around Nathalie. She was standing on the steeple, grinning up at him.

She had known he was coming. Of course she had. And she had given…or awoken…powers in her followers.

With the extra power of those minds, she was so strong. She was unbeatable.

He fell towards her. He was as helpless as a kitten.

The church snapped up towards him. Nathalie reached out a languid hand.

She plucked him out of the air as easily as if she were picking a flower.

Her hand clutched his throat, and an instant later the steeple was being sheared in two, as the vast energy of his fall was transmitted through Nathalie's body and out into the structure of the church. Fragments of white wood exploded around them, then his body was being turned in the air and he was hurtling down, down, down.

The ground jumped up to meet him, and then he was smashing into the earth.

This time, it was Jason who took the brunt of the impact. This time it was Nathalie who landed on top, having flipped the momentum of his fall with the adroitness of a juggler.

Pain coursed through him, and his mouth was full of blood.

《《——》》

S/he had done it! Ben felt a wave of joy flutter through his ten bodies.

It had been so easy. Slipping the energy of their minds forward, feeding it to Nathalie the way she had commanded.

It felt good to serve. It felt so good.

The power coursing through him/them had been an end in itself. It was the pure, beautiful essence of life.

He wanted more.

The clock was ticking. He could see it quite clearly in his mind's eye.

Not long now, and then…

…then there would be a flash of light, and all the energy he could ask for would be his.

All they had to do now was deal with the other one. The one floating gently out of the sky.

《《——》》

Jason could not breathe. A terrible weight was crushing his chest.

He opened his eyes, and saw her face. Her hair fluttered in the breeze. She was so beautiful.

She was standing on his chest.

Then she moved to one side, but still he couldn't breathe.

It wasn't her body that was crushing him, he realized. It was her mind.

He was full of the buzz of her thoughts. He could not shut her out. It was jagged and broken and awful.

Then he saw something move above her head, and a flash of hope shot through him.

She hasn't seen him, he thought, as Blake floated down out of the sky. He would land very close to them, he realized. *There's still a chance.*

He tried to call the thoughts back, but of course, it was too late.

Nathalie laughed, and she didn't even bother to look over her shoulder.

"No, you didn't give it away," she told him. He realized he had no idea if she was speaking aloud or in his thoughts. "I have sensed your approach. I knew you were coming before you even reached land. And I was ready for you."

Jason tried to scream, but not a sound came out.

Blake hit the ground with a jolt, but there was no pain.

He felt as light as a feather. He was full of peace.

There had been a moment of discomfort, as he had been aware of the strain of…of *something* pushing up from the woman beneath him, felt the *snap snap snap* of defences he hadn't even known he had possessed being sheared one after another.

And then he had been hers. It was so simple.

Why had he wanted to fight her, anyway?

He pulled out his knife, his special knife, and hacked away the corpse of the parachute.

Then he stepped forward and stood beside the slender woman with the dark hair. She looked at him with her endless black eyes.

Blake's hand tightened around the hilt of the dagger.

His eyes went to the figure sprawled on the floor.

«««—»»»

Ben frowned, and suddenly the weight of Nathalie was... lessened.

He could still feel her. Her mind was all around him, it was like a blanket that stretched over his thoughts...but she was no longer bent on him.

She's having to work hard on someone else, Ben realized.

Experimentally, he tried to move his head to see what was going on.

To his surprise, he found it was easy.

She can't hear me.

Ben looked at the church. Through the open doorway, he could see a blur of faces.

The whole town was in there. Everyone he had known.

Everyone he had ever loved.

Suddenly, it was all clear to him.

Gently, moving with a delicacy he had not known he possessed, he explored backwards along the mental path that Nathalie had opened between them. He found her other nine disciples. They were still focused completely on the task Nathalie had given them. He could feel the mind they were trying to hold in place. It was taking more effort than Nathalie had anticipated. It was taking a lot of her concentration, too.

Ben issued a command. It was easier than he had imagined.

Moving quietly, not even knowing why they were doing it, the other nine disciples began to move towards the bus.

Ben began moving too, but in a different direction.

He did not have long.

«««—»»»

205

THE FALL OF THE ANGEL NATHALIE

The dagger was wreathed in darkness. It fell towards Jason, and Jason screamed.

This was it. He couldn't breathe, he couldn't move, he couldn't...

But he could move.

Something had shifted, something had lessened, some mote of force that had been thrown against him was no loner there.

Jason bunched his legs and kicked as hard as he could.

He flew backwards, away from Nathalie, away from the church, away from the young man with the vacant eyes and the dark blade.

The dagger flashed through the air.

Jason landed awkwardly and tried to run.

But Nathalie was on him, bearing him down.

She was laughing. He could hear the steady tramp of footsteps as Blake drew near again.

《《—》》

Ben reached the church, and stared in through the door.

There was no way he could get inside in time. It was so full of people. It was awful. They had lain themselves down willingly, and were piled five deep in places.

How can the ones on the bottom breathe?

It was no good. How could he get there in time?

He could feel the seconds ticking away. He had less than a minute.

Then he felt her.

It was just the faintest flicker of awareness, but he was sure it was her.

His mother was down there. She was being crushed to death.

And near to her, so close she could almost reach out and touch it, the package ticked away.

No, Ben almost screamed.

He would not let this happen. Not after all the things he had done. All the things she had made him do.

He reached out to his mother...

206

…and felt her mind reach back to him.

Pass it to me, he told her.

Pass it to me, he told them all.

For an instant, he thought he had gone too far. Nathalie must have heard him, she *must* have…

But no.

She was further off, now. Her attention was on the two she was playing with.

Ben could still do it, if he was quick.

Pass it to me, he said again, more confidently.

They were doing it. He felt the package being picked up and passed from one hand to another.

They were helping him. The whole town was helping him.

And then it was being held out to him.

He reached out, and grasped it. It was only small, but it was so heavy.

A red digital display glared out at him.

It read 00:00:20.

As he watched, the numbers ticked away.

He had no more time to think. He had no more time to be quiet.

He shouldered the package, and began running awkwardly for the bus.

«««—»»»

Nathalie held him, with her hands and with her mind.

Jason could not move.

Blake drew closer. There was nothing on his face. Not a smile, not a glimmer of recognition, nothing.

Nathalie drew backwards, giving Blake room to move.

His hand went up again.

Behind their backs, Jason saw a figure dash desperately from the church.

A sudden, unreasonable, unthinking flash of hope welled up in him.

The figure was running towards the bus.

He reached the door and dove inside.

"Goodbye, Jason," said Nathalie. She sounded almost bored.

«‹—››»

Ben's arms screamed at him.

Each step, he knew he was going to fall.

If he tripped, he knew that he would not have a second chance.

The bus got closer and closer…and then the doors were in front of him, and he was throwing himself on board. As he hit the deck, he felt nine pairs of eyes snap down and fasten on him.

A faint surge of curiosity went up from them; and in response, he felt a twinge of alarm echo back from Nathalie. She knew something was wrong, but it was too late.

He had done it.

He reached out to his mother, and felt their minds touch once last time.

I'm sorry, he screamed at her.

I'm sorry and I love you and I love you I love you I lo…

«‹—››»

Jason saw her eyes flicker with doubt, and then half the world was on fire.

One moment the bus was there, the next a fireball of orange brilliance was rising into the sky.

And with a great *whooshing* noise as if he were on a train bursting out of a tunnel, the terrible weight was gone.

Her little toys were dead. The figure that had run for the bus…

Her soldiers had rebelled. And with their death, the unstoppable weight of their minds had been lifted.

Nathalie was reeling backwards, a look of horror on her face.

Now, thought Jason.

Now is the moment.

Blake sensed it, too. He was turning, shaking his head as the mental chains came loose.

Jason saw him turn to Nathalie, saw the look of realisation flash over his face, saw the determination form in his eyes.

This was it. He was going to kill her.

And Jason suddenly understood that he could not let that happen. He never could have.

He still loved her.

He would not let Blake kill her. Whatever would happen after would happen. But he would not stand by and let her die.

He tried to get up.

He could not move. He was too weak. He was too broken.

Even now, Nathalie's will was locked on his. He could feel her hate and malice pulsing through the mental connection she had opened up between them.

Blake was about to kill her, and he could do nothing to stop it.

He opened his mouth to scream.

And stopped. He could feel the object in his breast pocket. The small crystal vial he had taken from his stores what seemed like a million years ago. The small crystal vial that he had somehow forgotten, somehow overlooked up until now.

The small crystal vial with the last dregs of Nathalie's higher soul.

Dredging up every last ounce of his strength, he reached in his jacket and pulled out the vial. He snapped off the top.

Blake was lifting the blade now. The darkness shimmered and writhed like a black snake.

Jason upended the vial, and gulped the contents down.

For a moment, he felt the fiery liquid light up his mind, his essence, his very soul...

...and then he was handing it to her, flinging it through the link she had opened up between them, giving her back the soul he had tricked from her.

The world seemed to freeze.

209

THE FALL OF THE ANGEL NATHALIE

Nathalie screamed and fell. Her back arched.

Blake paused, standing over her.

Nathalie opened her eyes, and Jason felt the breath lodge in his throat.

Her eyes were not black any more. Nor were they the poisoned yellow of a daemon.

They were *her* eyes again, brown-green and beautiful and perfect.

They looked so sad.

Stop him, Jason screamed at her. *Use what I have given you! You can stop him from killing you*!

He knew that she had heard him.

For a moment her eyes flickered to Blake, and Jason saw the young man's knees buckle as she fixed him with her will.

Then she turned back to Jason. She smiled once, sadly.

Thank you, she told him.

Then she let go of Blake's mind and closed her eye.

The dark blade fell through the air.

It tore through her flesh as if Nathalie was made of shadows.

Jason had time to scream, time to see Blake pull the blade out, time to see the dark blood well up from her broken body and spill into the night.

Then the brightness of her mind went blank, and Jason began to weep.

«« — »»

It was a month later. The days were drawing in and Christmas was in the air.

Winter wind blew through the crowded boulevards of Covent Garden, but the two figures who sat on the bench were only thinly dressed. A few passers-by gave them curious glances; but there was a lot to look at here, and two under-dressed crazies were not high on the list.

The one who was not wearing dark glasses turned to the other.

"I thought that I'd be more happy," he said in a strange, flat voice.

The man in the dark glasses shrugged.

Jason looked thinner than he had done, more used up. But when he smiled there was something honest that Blake thought was new; and after all, he had not eaten anything for several weeks, and a certain hollowness was to be expected.

"What do you feel?" he asked.

Blake looked at him for a long time.

"I feel like I need something to keep me occupied," he said at last. It was true. He felt empty. He felt like he needed something to live for...or else he would not live. It was that simple.

He tried to shake the feeling off, and turned to Jason.

"What did they say?" Blake asked.

Jason shrugged.

"They tried to dissuade me, of course," he said. "The High Darkness even went so far as to say he had great expectations for me. I didn't take him too seriously. I have a rule about that: never get too chummy with someone who has recently threatened to eat your soul."

Blake smiled thinly.

"They won't try and stop you?" he asked.

Jason spread his hand.

"Well, we have this rule about something called *Intervention*, you see," he said. "Perhaps you've heard of it? Anyway, it cuts two ways. The High Darkness wasn't happy, but what can he do? Besides," he added gloomily, "I'm sure he will win a few of them back. All the more for him, at the end of the day."

Blake nodded. He supposed it was true.

"And what about you?" he said, when the silence had got too long.

"Me?" mused Jason, as if he hadn't considered the question. "Well, it was a bit off a toss up between going into acting, opening up a small patisserie in the south of France, and giving up my life of sin in exchange for a slow fading away to nothing that can only result in my eventual death as a way of somehow attempting to make amends for my wicked existence."

He shook his head sadly.

"A shame really. I really am very good at baking."

Jason sighed, and lifted up a small rucksack that he had brought with him.

He handed it over to Blake, who opened it, looked at the contents for a moment, then zipped it back up.

"There's a little book in the front pouch," Jason explained. "I was always meticulous with my records. Also, there's an envelope with some cash and a passport. Turns out my storage space was worth a pretty penny. And I know you'll need ah, travelling expenses." He rolled his eyes sheepishly. "I did get around, after all."

"Thanks," said Blake.

Jason paused. People came and went. The wind blew, and Jason shivered.

"I should be going then," he said.

He got up.

"Make it worthwhile," Jason said. "And tell them I'm sorry. That, too, if you don't mind."

He started to walk away.

"Wait," Blake called after him, and Jason halted. He turned and lifted one eyebrow quizzically.

"We're not friends, nothing like that," Blake told him awkwardly. "I was never wrong about you. I always knew exactly what you were." He paused, unsure how to go on.

Jason looked at him flatly.

"But thanks for not telling me the third difference," Blake said at last. "Between us, I mean. I knew it anyway. Thanks for not rubbing it in my face."

Jason nodded.

"Have a good life," he said. Then he shrugged. "Who knows? Maybe I'll see you on the other side. Maybe there's still room for that."

He turned away, and he was gone.

People streamed past, hundreds of them.

Blake had never felt more alone.

He opened the rucksack, pulled out the book Jason had mentioned, and started flicking through it.

Oh well. He supposed he had to start somewhere.

‹‹‹—›››

Jason opened a door into a dark place, and stepped through.

Daemonhearth stretched away into the distance, red and thin and awfully, horribly empty.

The door closed behind him.

He took a lungful of the tasteless air, then held his breath, listening quietly. There was not the faintest echo of noise anywhere. He had come to the furthest, most abandoned corner of Daemonhearth that he could get to. It was hardly even a place, more of a possibility.

Well, this was it.

He started walking, going even further.

He thought of the last thing Blake had said to him.

He decided he would hold onto that, if he could. It was a good last thought to have, as everything he was, everything he had ever been slowly melted away.

It was true. Laura had never loved Blake. But there had been a time, many hundreds and hundreds of years ago, when Jason had loved Nathalie. And she had loved him back.

Whatever had happened afterwards.

She had loved him.

Jason put one foot in front of the other.

After a long, long time, he still wasn't nothing.

He wasn't nothing, but he was close.

EPILOGUE

"All done," said June, smiling through her awful teeth at the happy American couple.

She held out the doll, and the woman took it from her.

She's pretty, June thought to herself. *Even with that scar on her cheek.*

She didn't feel jealous. She had gotten over being jealous of pretty women a long time ago. Even women who were pretty *and* pregnant.

"Thank you so much," the woman gushed. "It was my mother's doll, you see. We wanted it to be perfect for the baby when it arrives, didn't we, Stan?"

The woman beamed up at her husband.

They looked very happy together.

"Yes, Julie's mother got it in England during the war," Stan told her. "And we've always wanted to come and visit. So we thought, what the hell…God knows we won't have another chance, once our little friend gets here…"

Stan trailed off and put a hand on his wife's belly.

June's smile widened a little.

"Do you know if it's a boy or a girl?" she asked.

215

The little bell above the door rung out, and June began leading them back out of the workroom and into the main shop.

"It's a girl," Julie told her happily.

"Lovely," said June, and she meant it. Either way she would have been happy, but a girl felt…right, somehow. "Have you thought of any names?"

A young man was waiting in the shop. He had a rucksack on his shoulders. He was obviously waiting politely for June to finish speaking to her clients. It looked like he wanted to talk to her.

"Oh, yes," said Stan. "We have one in mind."

"We want to name her after someone who helped us once," Julie went on, then stopped as she realized there was another customer waiting. "But never mind that. We can see you're busy. Thanks so much for your help! How much do we owe you?"

June waved the offer of money away, as she always did in such cases.

"Don't be silly," she told them. "I hope your little girl likes it. I'm sure she will. Enjoy your stay!"

The couple smiled at her again, and the bell rang as they left the shop.

June turned her attention to the young man.

"Hello," she said. "Are you looking for anything in particular?"

The young man smiled, and reached into his backpack.

"Actually," he told her, "I think I have something that belongs to you."

JAMIE BRINDLE has been writing stories for many years. Occasionally, they are even published.

He was raised by two ex-hippies that sold boomerangs for a living and grew a hedge maze in their back garden, in Bedfordshire, England. He was home educated until the age of fourteen, which gave him lots of time to do the really important things in life, like make boomerangs and run around mazes.

He studied biochemistry at the University of Susses, before realising that he didn't really enjoy working in labs. He then worked in a school for around four years—a terrifying experience for someone who was home educated—before studying medicine at Warwick University. He currently works as a GP trainee in the East Midlands. He finds writing speculative fiction a wonderful way to unwind after long shifts spent in the bizarre fantasy world of the NHS.

This is his first published novel. Shorter stories are available online. If you really like them, you can even buy a collection.

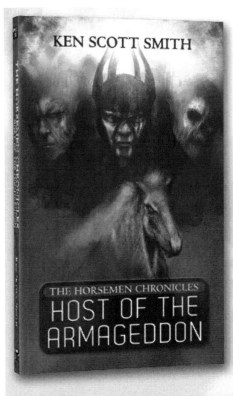

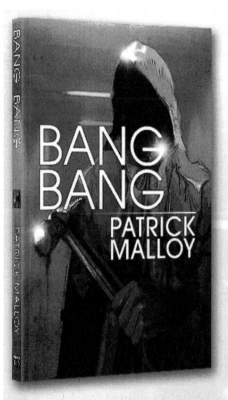

LETTERS FROM HADES

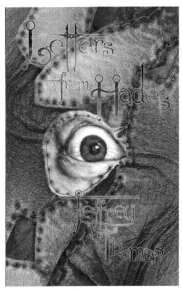

A man awakens in Hell where he is schooled in the ways of the damned. And once educated, he is released to wander Hell on his own. He journeys from one city to the next, dodging demon patrols and avenging angels hunting the damned for sport. Along the way to the city of Oblivion, he discovers a band of rebellious damned have left a tortured and beautiful demon to rot. He rescues her and sets in motion a series of events that could lead to the final battle between Heaven and Hell, angel and demon, demon and damned.

LETTERS FROM HADES is a travelogue of Hell — a world not that far from the very world we live in now. It is a story of rebellion, a story of love and a story of hope and rebirth set in a beautifully dark and textured world brought to brilliant life by Jeffrey Thomas, the acclaimed author of PUNKTOWN.

WWW.NECROPUBLICATIONS.COM

JEFFREY THOMAS

Printed in Great Britain
by Amazon.co.uk, Ltd.,
Marston Gate.